PROMISE OF THE GUN

Bob Archer was determined to draw a line under the past—his days as a leader of vigilantes were over and he was going to settle down to a farmer's life with his brother Ray. However, no sooner had he settled into his brother's home than all hell broke loose! With his brother lying wounded by a coward's bullet, Archer vowed he wouldn't let Manderson succeed. Now he faced a desperate fight for survival knowing that an evil past could not be shaken off and that the promise of the gun was death.

PROMISE OF THE GUN

PROMISE OF THE GUN

by
Sam Gort

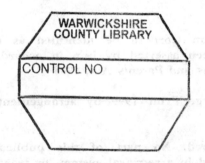

Dales Large Print Books
Long Preston, North Yorkshire,
England.

British Library Cataloguing in Publication Data.

Gort, Sam
  Promise of the gun.

  A catalogue record for this book is
  available from the British Library

  ISBN 1-85389-948-8 pbk

First published in Great Britain by Robert Hale Ltd., 1998

Cover illustration © Prieto by arrangement with Norma Editorial S.A.

Published in Large Print 1999 by arrangement with Robert Hale Ltd.

Dales Large Print is an imprint of
Library Magna Books Ltd.
Printed and bound in Great Britain by
T.J. International Ltd., Cornwall, PL28 8RW.

ONE

Bob Archer settled as deeply as he could into the cushions on the seat of brother Ray's rocking chair. Gazing out from the veranda which ran across the front of the Archer farmhouse, he took in the rolling, rock-crested scene beyond him and reckoned this part of north Texas took some beating. It was beautiful, the atmosphere was clear and bright into the farthest yonder, and the air itself had the taste of wine. Perfect; and it was years since Archer had felt this relaxed and at peace with himself.

But then that was what this spell of rest was all about. He was played-out and needed a few days of complete inactivity to get over the accumulated hurts and stresses of a decade in the saddle and living hard.

One way and another, he had taken a fair beating during the last ten years. He had fought for the South right through the war and into the frightful peace which had followed it. The Yankees had done terrible things down this way—a harvest of murder, sickness, poverty, ruin, and suicide being all they'd encouraged—and Bob Archer felt not the smallest twinge of conscience about having formed the Sadd River Vigilantes in the June of 1865 and gone into the business of bringing justice where carpetbag law had brought nothing but wrongs that had been impossible to stomach.

Everywhere you'd turned in those months and years directly after the surrender, corruption had been rife and the strong had ruled without mercy. Somebody with the guts, will, and imagination had had to do something—even when it had meant bucking the efforts of the often misdirected Texas Rangers themselves—and Archer had been that man. He and his boys—often by night and bearing fire—had carried rough justice across the plains of Texas and righted wrongs according to their lights. It had been done in the name and memory of the Old South, and Archer had no regrets. But now it was over, and the Sadd River Vigilantes had been disbanded. By this spring of 1872, bad law had been largely replaced by good and injustice had receded to a tolerable level. This was not a perfect world—never had been such, and never would. There was a point at which idealism became vindictiveness and vindictiveness revenge, while revenge became a new rebellion that threatened to suck in a rising generation as yet unfamiliar with the horrors of war. Bob Archer wanted none of that. He had never been about anything but what was best for folk—and accepted wholeheartedly that to live was to strive and suffer, because that was what it was inevitably taken up with—and now he was ready to share the common task and seek a future of his own.

Strictly within the law, and by courtesy of his brother Ray for a start.

Archer dozed as the sun touched his face. He dreamed of pretty girls, picnic mosses, and rustling woods. It was all sylvan and idyllic—perhaps a little too close to Man's fabled view of heaven—and Archer wakened abruptly on the grunting edge of a snore, his eyes shocking open and his spine bracing sharply against the back of his chair and setting the rocker vigorously in motion. Suddenly his every sense was alert and he was inwardly reaching for his gun and looking for a horse that wasn't there. What the deuce was up? It seemed that he had just been kicked out of heaven and landed on the all too familiar edge of hell.

He peered towards the heave of the eastern skyline, his eyes, dimmed by his minutes of near-sleep, straining at detail, but he could make out nothing amiss on the vast spread of land before him. After that he looked southwards, seeing ground that was also clear, and then north, where he perceived sudden movement—that of his brother's farm waggon heaving out of a low which was little more than a furrow in the earth and coming on apace, young Harry, his nephew, a boy of thirteen, driving the two pulling horses at a speed that was too great and with a skill that was too little, for he lacked a man's strength as yet.

Archer thrust himself to his feet. Hurrying to the end of the veranda on his left, he slapped his palms down on the retaining rail and watched anxiously as the waggon rushed towards the farmhouse, rumbling audibly now, and coming on in a bumping crescendo of sound that ended in a fuming, brake-assisted halt opposite the steps which led down at the front centre of the veranda into the limed and dusty yard space where the hens clucked and scratched in their daily search for worms that were seldom there.

Turning away from the veranda's end

rail, Archer ran back in the direction of the steps, calling his nephew's name; but then he saw what the recent dangerous haste had been all about, for his brother Ray was sitting doubled forward in the back of the vehicle and obviously hurt as a great deal of fresh blood was spread around him on the waggon's floor. Now, craning towards the open front door of the dwelling at his back, Archer shouted: 'Anne! Get out here pronto! It's your husband, girl! Ray's been hurt!'

Archer didn't wait for a reply, but jumped down off the veranda—clearing the steps—and went to the rear of the waggon, where young Harry had already lowered the tailgate and was reaching out to help his injured father, who was creeping awkwardly towards him on doubled knees and looking both dazed and pain-racked. Archer paused for a split second then, putting the boy aside, scrambled into the vehicle's back and steadied his crawling brother with both hands, at the same time glancing at his nephew and asking: 'What happened, Harry? Your pa's been shot! How the dickens did that happen? You and him were doing no more wrong than take the water barrel out to Cold Wells for a fill-up!'

'Don't bother the boy with it, Bob,' the shot man gasped. 'He's done better than well already. It—it was Manderson's men. They showed up while me and Harry was there. Tug Filby, Manderson's foreman, put a bullet in me when I—I—'

'You what, Ray?'

'I reached for my Winchester.'

'What did you go and do that for?'

'Seemed appropriate.'

'Why in hell?'

'They said we couldn't have any water— and tipped out what we had got. Then busted the barrel up.'

'Why wouldn't they let you have any water?' Archer demanded, lowering his brother over the back of the waggon from the armpits and easing him down inch by inch until his feet settled on the ground. 'Ray, I never heard of such a thing!'

'Yes, you have,' the wounded man retorted waspishly. 'What's new, Bob? Water's not short in these parts—just hereabouts—and Orville Manderson wants the lot for those damned beeves of his.' He shook his head impatiently as his brother Bob threatened again to run on indignantly. 'This is no concern of yours, mister. But it's been in the wind for some while.'

'Since old Shamus Manderson himself died a few months ago,' a woman's voice put in.

Raising his eyes, Bob Archer saw that his sister-in-law, Anne, a pretty, dark-haired woman in her middle thirties, had arrived from inside the house and was reaching out to take her husband from him and thus free his hands to help him make his own descent from the tail of the waggon. 'Go on,' Archer encouraged, jumping down to the ground.

'Old Shamus's son, Orville,' the woman

continued, 'the new owner of the Broken M ranch by inheritance—that's up there on the high ground to the north of us—has been throwing his weight about everywhere he goes. People have to put up with it—because he's got the money and power to back up his evil ways—and we've tried to put up with it too. But we've got so much more to lose than most. The water at Cold Wells is absolutely vital to us and the other farms about us. We all draw from the wells, and our stock drinks there.'

'Ain't it a sin!' Ray Archer acknowledged, his long and muscular body pulling out of his wife's grasp as he sank to the ground and sat among the chicken droppings, his pale-skinned, blue-eyed face turned up to his brother's and the patches of baldness on his blond pate catching the sun. 'This I could surely have done without, Bob. Right in the middle of the spring sowing. Have a look at where that slug hit me. You're the man who's seen all the bullet-wounds. How bad is—is it?'

'It ain't good,' Bob Archer responded, squatting beside his brother and carefully doing what had been asked of him, 'and that's for sure. Looks to me like your shoulder-bone has been busted. Chipped at best.' He felt behind the injury, the tips of his fingers passing over the top of Ray's back. 'If that was only the worst of it!'

'What else, Bob?' Anne Archer inquired tensely.

'The bullet's still in there,' her brother-in-law replied. 'It'll have to be cut out from behind. Want me to do it?'

'Like hell you will!' Ray snorted disdainfully. 'You were always too handy with a shut-knife when we were kids. You keep your paws off!'

'Well—sure,' Bob Archer said doubtfully. 'If you want to go on suffering. That wound must hurt. Picked up one like it myself at—But never mind that.'

'Never mind it indeed!' Ray's wife agreed severely, her gaze withering the second man for a moment. 'Harry!' This to her gangling, yellow-haired son, and sharply. 'Go and get your pony out. Ride over to Starrville. Tell Doctor John Haste that your pa has been shot. Ask him to come out here as quickly as he can.'

'Yes, Ma,' the son said dutifully, and turned away, running towards the rear of the farmhouse and the stables situated there which could not be seen from the front of the dwelling.

'We'd better get you indoors, Ray,' Bob Archer said, studying his brother thoughtfully. 'I'd put your weight at about one-fifty. That's not too much for me to carry. Will you let me pick you up?'

'I'll let you help me up,' the wounded man sniffed, goggle-eyed and ashen with shock and weakness.

'I don't think that'll do it, brother,' Bob Archer said, giving his head a slow and judicious shake. 'Those legs of yours will buckle like rusty tin if you try to stand on them again.'

'Let him carry you, Ray,' the man's wife

ordered crisply. 'Stop behaving like a pair of children.'

'You heard her, kid,' Ray said ironically but without a hint of further argument.

Bob, the younger of the pair by a year or two and much the bigger man, got one arm under his brother's thighs and circled Ray's body with the other, lifting his virtually deadweight sibling as if the older brother weighed almost nothing at all and then carrying him up the veranda steps and into the living-room of the farmhouse, where he halted with Ray flop-limbed and near fainting in his grasp while his sister-in-law rounded him and walked to a door in the room's back wall and opened the way into the master bedroom beyond. 'Put him on the bed, please,' Anne urged, stepping aside and indicating the clear path with a sweep of her hand.

Bob Archer crossed the threshold on the woman's left. He saw the bed standing white and without a wrinkle before him. Hesitating, he craned at the female who had entered in his wake and said: 'You sure about putting him on the bed, Anne? He's a fair old mess, you know. Wouldn't it be best to put him in that raffia chair yonder and clean him up first?'

'You're shilly-shallying, Bob,' his sister-in-law accused.

'There may not be too much water to do the washing in,' Archer reminded. 'That's what I was thinking.'

'It's his bed,' Anne Archer said firmly. 'Put him on it.'

'Yes, ma'am,' Bob acknowledged resignedly, then stepped up to the bed and lowered his injured brother on to the snow-white counterpane. 'How're you doing, soldier?'

'With your thick skull and those muscles,' came the response, 'I figure I'll get rid of the team and harness you to the plough instead.'

'All brawn and no brain,' Bob Archer said cheerfully. 'That's me okay. Didn't Ma always say?'

'Some days we had down in the Big Bend,' his brother agreed, smiling, then fainted off.

'Is he going to die?' Anne asked bleakly, her lips quivering slightly as she gazed down on her husband from the foot of the bed.

Bob Archer shook his head uncertainly. 'That ain't normally a mortal wound, Annie, but a forty-four calibre slug fired from close range surely arrives with a hell of a smack! He's in shock. Reckon he's strong enough, though. Yeah, he'll make it.' He paused. 'Boil some water, and bring your scissors in. We'll have to cut the shirt off him. That and a clean up is about all we should attempt. Just make him as comfortable as we can. The rest of it is work for the doctor.'

'Pray God John Haste gets here before too long,' Anne Archer said, turning away from the foot of the bed and re-entering the living room. 'To think—I was a happy woman an hour ago.'

'Sure,' Bob agreed rather absently, 'the big troubles always seem to come out of nowhere. Where are those scissors?'

The scissors were soon supplied, and after that a basin of hot water was brought through from the kitchen. Then Archer and his sister-in-law spent half an hour working on the wounded man in a concentrated fashion; and, when the blood-soaked garments had been fully removed from Ray's upper body and his injury cleaned and staunched, Bob straightened up from his laving and dropped the lump of cotton waste which he had been using into the red waters of the bowl beside him, sighing heavily. Then he picked up a towel and began drying his hands with the same slow care which he had shown in his every action just recently, the sun-coarsened flesh of his middle brow nipping inwards upon the straight bone and wide nostrils of a nose that was only matched in character by the dark block of the jaw beneath it. Now he said firmly: 'Annie, this has got to be nipped in the bud.'

It was a rather bald statement, for little had been voiced in the last three-quarters of an hour, but the woman's mind seemed to have been tracking his own, since her next words proved that she knew exactly what he meant. 'Bob, it's up and running.'

'Then we have to put a stopper on it,' he responded grimly, looking her straight in the eyes. 'It's up to us.'

Anne Archer began filling her lungs audibly, and she went on drawing air until her chest could hold no more. She was clearly trying to control emotions that were just too deeply felt to be controlled, and suddenly her anger and bitterness burst from her in words of the greatest savagery. 'I didn't want you here, Bob Archer. I told Ray I didn't want you here. I begged him not to let you come. You're trouble! You're a self-righteous, gabby hypocrite! You think you and that gang of yours did wonderful things for the people of the South, but it was all for you in reality. Your pride! The war was over, and enough people had died, but you had to go on with the killing and stir up more hatred.' She wetted her lips, plainly seeking the most hurtful words and phrases in a verbal armoury that was not understocked. 'The South lost the war. You and the army you fought with were defeated. In my view, Bob, that was a just outcome. It wasn't a good war, and we were in the wrong. Don't talk to me about the free land issue; that was just an excuse to keep the black people in the fields. Had you and all those like you been the folk you believed yourselves to be, you'd have accepted that from the start and realized that the Stars and Bars were false and you never had a cause. The defeat was honourable and its terms the same. Robert E. Lee himself said so. But you and your so-called vigilantes were without honour and couldn't accept the peace. You'd lived in blood and breathed powdersmoke for too long. Now you declare your mission achieved and yourself made over—a new man, full of hope and peaceful desires. What nonsense! You didn't disband those gangsters of yours because you believed that you and they were strong in the right and had done all that you could. No, sir! I'll tell you why you disbanded that Sadd River scum. You did it because the law was breathing down your neck and you could feel the trap in the gallows floor shaking under your feet. You've given up playing God and Jeff Davis, brother-in-law, but you've brought the shadow of your wickedness with you to Ray Archer's farm. You're still hunting trouble, and it seems you've once again found it. Or it's found you!' She swallowed hard and blinked back a tear. 'That's your brother lying there—as good a man as they come—and you don't seem to care a fig for the poor fellow!'

'You finished?' Bob Archer inquired evenly, trying to keep all trace of the shame and pain that she had caused him out of his voice and face.

'No, I haven't!' she flared, reaching across the bed on which her husband still lay unconscious and slapping her brother-in-law hard on the left cheek. 'I want you out of here and hundreds of miles away!'

'Why?' he asked in reasonable tones, gently rubbing the flesh which her flying palm had reddened.

'Why?' Anne Archer echoed. 'You have the effrontery to ask me that!'

'Tell me.'

'I'm sure you're going to make trouble around here on the pretext of helping us!' the dark woman answered.

'Haven't you got trouble then?' Bob Archer inquired. 'Ray lying there ain't trouble?'

Anne Archer gestured hopelessly, crying openly now. 'Yes,' her brother-in-law sighed, 'it's trouble all right, and we both know it. Nor does it have a blind thing to do with the Civil War or the Sadd

River Vigilantes. The trouble we have here is the plain, old fashioned, everyday kind. The sort ornery people make, and we have to take care of ourselves. Not that it had a heap to do with me, as of yesterday, I do declare, but I'm butting in today. I'll be doing it for Ray and the boy—and not for a woman who hates my guts for reasons she probably don't fully understand herself. You hear me, Anne? I promise you I'll do my best by them, and I won't let anything you have to say deter me.'

'The only promise you're making, Bob Archer,' the woman insisted, 'is the promise of the gun. The promise of the gun is death.'

He pulled a slight jib, wishing he could somehow refute that; but the truth could never be a lie.

TWO

Bob Archer dipped into the breastpocket of his shirt and fished out the 'makings'. Standing there, he calmly built himself a smoke, while his sister-in-law went on crying to herself; then, putting the cigarette in his mouth, he rummaged out a match and struck the sulphur tip with a flick of his thumbnail, touching off his rolled tobacco as fire flared and sucking deeply, then letting the inhaled smoke reappear in a rush from his mouth and nostrils. 'Dirty habit,' he said, more to himself than the woman. 'No good to a man. But I take pleasure in it.'

'Because that's the kind of man you are,' his sister-in-law gulped disdainfully.

'No doubt, no doubt,' he conceded. 'I haven't claimed to be much, but you see me as even less. But that's of little account.' He flicked the first of his ash into the bloody bowl near his right ankle. 'Anne—will you go and sit down in that raffia chair?'

'Why?'

'Because I need to talk to you. Stop worrying about Ray. We've done all we can for him just now.'

The woman walked to the raffia chair and lowered herself into it, settling tiredly. 'What is it?' she asked, brushing at her eyes with the back of her right hand and then staring up at him defiantly. 'What is it you want?'

'I said "need". There is a difference, you know.'

'That from a man who can barely read and write.'

'I don't know what's up with you,' Archer said frankly, 'but don't make this harder than it has to be. We are family.'

She nodded. 'All right.'

'How long have you lived here?'

'Going on six years. Since Ray mustered out.'

'And you've had no trouble over Cold Wells before this?'

'None. I told you about old Shamus Manderson. He could be trusted to stick to any agreement he made.'

'There is—or was—an actual agreement concerning those wells then?'

Her chin jerked again.

'The signed and sealed sort?'

'It was notarized, yes.'

'There are two parts to an agreement—right?'

'In a case like this—yes.'

'Where's your part?'

'At the next farm to the west of us,' the woman answered, her shape firming up a little in her chair. 'The Luker place. Jack Luker's.'

'What does the agreement actually cover?' Archer queried. 'There's got to be something more to it than the water. It seems to me the boundary factor would cover that in the great majority of cases.'

'Well, yes,' the woman admitted, 'and that's the devil of it. Cold Wells lie at the foot of the high ground which forms the Manderson range and was originally part of the Broken M, as claimed.'

'Hell,' Archer muttered, dragging hard at his cigarette and exhaling almost at once in the same fashion, 'that puts a different complexion on it. Or appears to. So the water was Manderson's in the first place.'

'Yes,' Anne Archer said, frowning, 'but the fact of it changes nothing that the agreement wasn't drawn up to take care of. The wells were of no use to Shamus Manderson in the ranching of his day. His cattle couldn't reach them without descending from the part of the ridge above the water by a roundabout path which was safer blocked off anyway. Besides, there's plenty of water up there and the Red River itself isn't that far from the Broken M ranch house to the north. But, whatever the practical drawbacks involved, Shamus Manderson was too good a businessman to leave any resource unused and he soon arrived at a way of using the wells to his advantage. The need for water down here was an obvious one, and the man who owned the lower land had something that he figured he could get in exchange for it.'

'Like what, Annie?'

'The thousand acres of prime grass at the eastern end of this strip of farmland.'

'Ah,' Archer grunted in a sudden moment of what amounted to profound insight. 'I see it now. As a matter of fact, I noticed it as I rode in here. The ridge to the north of us settles eastwards and links up with the grass you've mentioned via a sort of landbridge which provides free passage back and forth for the cattle which belong on the high range. Manderson let the farmers down here have the water in Cold Wells in exchange for that right of passage. Correct?'

'Absolutely, Bob.'

'It occurs to me,' Archer mused, 'that this farmland must all have been graze at one time. On the laws of the business, it would almost certainly have been claimed as such.'

'You have a ready grasp of these things,' his sister-in-law admitted grudgingly. 'I can't give the full history of it; if you want that you'll have to seek it of somebody else; but, as I've heard Ray tell it, a man named Peter Blood claimed this low land in the late Eighteen-forties—shortly after Shamus Manderson himself appeared in these parts and began rearing cattle for the old hide-and-tallow business—and Blood's intention was to follow Manderson's example. But then, however, the water problem came up and Peter Blood decided that this lower ground would do better under the plough anyhow, as it had become apparent to him that his land got drier and drier the further to the south he rode. He had ideas at first of digging wells and irrigating—if you can imagine it—but that costs money and he decided to defray the costs he foresaw by inviting interested parties to take out mortgages and join him in his farming venture. It sounded all right—and even looked all right on paper—but in fact it was too big for the men of that time to handle, and Manderson's water—so convenient to the lower ground that it ought to have belonged to it, in the property sense, from the beginning—provided the simpler solution to the farming body and was readily taken up, especially as that grass to the east was so far out from the main body of the Blood holding that nobody wanted to work it anyhow. The arrangement wasn't perfect, I guess—as the written agreement was proof of—but there was trust enough between the parties and everybody went to work with a will.'

'A situation that appears to have existed, until this, ever since,' Archer observed.

'Yes,' the woman said heavily. 'The land along this northern edge of the Blood country is good land and it isn't difficult to make a fair living from it.'

'Given that the access to Cold Wells remains?'

'Obviously.'

'I take it that Peter Blood is dead? You told me that Jack Luker holds the water agreement.'

'Jack was Peter Blood's heir. Peter died just before the war started. He never married.'

'Thank you,' Archer said. 'I now have a clear picture of how it was. I figure I know all too well how it is.'

'Let it lie.'

'I can't let it lie.'

'You'll only stir up real trouble with the Broken M,' Anne Archer pleaded bitterly. 'Orville Manderson can be a mean, hard man, and that son of his, young Jem, is no better. In fact he could even be worse. He's been raised to believe that the Manderson will is law, and that he can do no wrong.' She checked momentarily, bringing her hands together in a loud clap. 'Please, Bob! Can't you see what we're up against?'

'Sure,' he said grimly. 'Story of my life, sister-in-law; and I still can't let it lie. If I don't pick up the gauntlet, somebody else will. Somebody much less experienced maybe.' He considered her critically for a long moment. 'How many of you farmers are there on the strip?'

'Six all told. Jack Luker, Timmy Dean, Ed Malone, Frank Balls, Bill Haines, and Sam Parker.'

'Any got families?'

'They all have.'

'Any got sons?'

'All have.'

'Grown up?'

'For the most part.'

'Sounds like quite a body of men.'

'That's what I'm most afraid of, Bob!' Anne Archer confessed intensely. 'You can't really give up the past—don't want to. The war gave you your real purpose

35

in life. You're a limited man otherwise! You see your fellows as men to be led into battle—gunfodder! You glory in it, and will look for any reason or excuse to keep it going! A woman can feel a man like you sucking at her spirit and everything that she knows to be good. How could I ever face bereaved mothers and widowed wives? All because of the folly that I know you want to lead others into! We've taken no pride in your wicked reputation and doings, Bob Archer! You have shamed your family!'

'You're at it again!' Archer declared, scowling his disdain at the floor and almost spitting after it. 'This is your house, and I don't want to abuse your hospitality, but you need to wise up plenty, woman! The world ain't never going to be how you want it to be just on account you want it so. No, ma'am! Do you figure all those farmers and their sons for gutless? I don't expect them to be so, and would plain hate it if they turned out like that.

If Manderson and his crowd are allowed to cordon off the water at Cold Wells, you and the folk around you are going to be left with a great big nothing. Can't you grasp what the Broken M is up to here? It's no new story! If you people can't get water, you'll have to leave this place—and with you gone, your farms will grass-over within a season or two. After that, Orville Manderson will be able to drive in a new herd down here, 'cos you can bet your bottom dollar that's his aim!'

'What kind of fools do you take us for?' the woman demanded. 'Do you imagine what you've just said is so clever we couldn't think of it? The possibility that you've just spoken of was always there. It's been discussed up and down the strip dozens of times. We had to trust and keep on trusting, but we were all mighty scared people during the months that old Shamus was failing. Things were said. Like the past was past and couldn't be allowed to count today. They're a covetous lot on the Broken M. But their badness is no reason why we should get killed. You can start over in your working life most any time, but you can't bring the dead back. If we have to give up here, there are other places we can go. I'd much rather that than see blood spilled and homes burning. After your lawless way of going to work!'

'Glad you're getting it all off your chest,' Archer said. 'You keep telling me you know what I'm going to do—even when you don't know. Forced to it, I'll operate anyhow I have to—that's a fact!—but you're assuming I'm going to step outside the law before first trying to settle this from inside it. That's where your mistake is, Annie. I get real angry at times and blow off steam, but I seldom lose my head. A legal document can be legally enforced.' He checked, drawing breath. 'Your local town is Starrville, isn't it?'

'Yes. What of it?'

'You've a sheriff in Starrville, haven't you?'

'Buck Stevens, yes.'

'Is he a good sheriff?'

'He's up to his job.'

'Up to forcing the Broken M to obey the law?'

'If it came to it, I think so, yes.'

'Sounds encouraging,' Archer acknowledged. 'So, if Jack Luker will ride into town with me and show the sheriff that water agreement from way back, I reckon that Manderson will realize that he can't do just what he likes around here and accept whatever constraints the sheriff puts on him.'

'Orv Manderson wants to repudiate his father's promises, that's plain.'

'He can't,' Archer said, 'and do it legal. The water agreement is a legal document. You told me so yourself. So there'll be a copy of it with the lawyer who acts as the town notary. A record anyhow. The son can't just deny his father's promises and start again. Ray and the other farmers should be able to rely on that.'

'Yet my husband was shot by Tug Filby,' Anne Archer reminded him.

'Ray admitted that he reached for his Winchester,' her brother-in-law pointed out in return. 'I daresay Filby would be able to make out a pretty good case of self-defence from that. But a bullet fired in anger by a foreman is no reason for being scared stiff of the guy's boss and giving up on the real case at trial.' He gave a chuckle that was brief and brittle. 'Seems to me we've switched sides somewhat—though I know we haven't. This has been a shock for you, Anne. Make allowances. Your neighbours will rally round.'

'All we've done is talk, Bob' the woman said. 'We've cured nothing.'

'Because we can't right here and now,' he temporised. 'But we've opened roads. That's the correct beginning.'

The man stretched out upon the bed stirred a little and groaned softly.

'Is he coming round?' Anne Archer enquired, starting to her feet.

'Sounds like it,' her brother-in-law answered, though he was listening far more acutely at the farmyard. 'I think your son's got back. I'll swear that was his pony coming in.'

'Go and see,' the woman said, stepping up to the bedside and bending over her husband.

Bob Archer walked back into the parlour. He saw at once that his hearing had not deceived him. His nephew, the gangling tow-haired Harry, had just come in through the front door. The boy was hot and anxious, and he gazed at his uncle with an unspoken question in his blue eyes.

'Your pa's all right,' Archer said. 'Where's the doc?'

'Driving here in his buggy, Uncle Bob.'

'Will he be long, Harry?'

'Ten minutes maybe. Perhaps a bit more.'

'Okay,' Archer said, nodding. 'You go

along and keep your ma company. I've a place I must go.'

'Where?'

Archer hesitated, but he did not suppose it would matter if he said. 'Jack Luker's farm. Your mother knows what my business there will be. She'll guess it anyhow.'

'Right you are, Uncle Bob,' Harry said. 'We sure got you out of the chair you were snugged down in, didn't we?'

'You sure as heck did!' Archer acknowledged, as the boy stepped past him and entered the bedroom where his wounded father lay.

Then Archer heard his sister-in-law and the boy start speaking together, and he walked out onto the veranda and stepped down into the farmyard, striding then round to the back of the dwelling—where the more important outbuildings were situated—and, after crossing further hard and dusty ground, he passed into the stables. His mount, a big black gelding with an intelligent head, stirred within its narrow stall and neighed almost pitifully at him. 'Yes, I know,' Archer soothed. 'This is no life for a tough old ranger like you. Want to be seeing what's over the next hill, eh? It's been hell-for-leather since the Junction. That's back a-piece, by heaven! Be damned if I'll let you pull a plough, suh. I'll sell you to a Texas riding man, that I will. But we've one more job first, and I've the feeling it could get sticky. You on?'

The horse tossed its head. It could even have known what he was saying. But his presence and the tone of his voice undoubtedly made it sure that it was about to get out of the stable, and that was sufficient unto its day. It backed up of its own accord when Archer removed the drop-rail, then shook itself loose and blew with relief as its master turned to the tack bench and picked up saddle and bridle. Finally, it stood like a rock and let him dress it for the trail.

After that Archer led the creature outside into the brightness of the day; then, with his hand at the bit, he walked beside its head until they were clear of the farm buildings, where he mounted up and, holding the now surging black in check, guided it on to the dirt track which ran westwards from here and appeared to connect all the farms along the strip. Almost at once Archer saw a horse and buggy bowling towards him and, touching his forelock to the vehicle's aquiline and grizzled driver—Doctor John Haste for a certainty, if his traditional black suit and medical bag were to be credited—kept well over to his right and then kneed his mount onwards, letting it pick up its hooves in a fast trot and grunt its pleasure in the exercise.

They followed the loom of the steep-faced ridge which crossed the land to the north of them. The frowning height created an overbearing presence against the flatness of the surrounding country, and Archer was reflecting that the scene was spoiled by its shadow, when a slight movement on the crest to his right plucked at the tail of his eye. He looked up and round, spotting a rider atop the summit yonder, but the horseman veered aside on the realization that he had been seen and sank from view, though the man below had no feeling that the other had gone away. Archer frowned to himself, his spine creeping a trifle. It seemed that he was being shadowed from the top of the ridge, and he judged from the apparent fact of it that his brother's farm was being watched. Well, now that he had been informed of what was happening locally, that did not surprise him too much. Though he couldn't think why in hell the watcher should want to actually trace his course. Was there trouble to come?

Archer slapped his right hip. He hadn't strapped on his gunbelt before leaving the house. Now that had been plumb foolish of him. It was madness to travel unarmed when the enemy had started shooting.

Perhaps his sister-in-law's plea that he refrain from violence had sunk deeper into his mind than he had supposed. That really would not do. This neck-of-the-woods was no place for pacifists!

THREE

Keeping half an eye raised to the north of him, Archer went on riding straight ahead. He felt more than half inclined to return to his brother's farm and arm himself before going further, yet believed that he would not be travelling far and could not fully credit that his presence hereabouts—that of an absolute newcomer as yet—was seriously threatened; so, shrugging indifferently and letting a certain recklessness carry the matter, he dismissed the impulse to caution and tried to think of other things, bringing a large thatched house and cluster of farm buildings into sight within the next minute or two and spotting a bulky figure clad in overalls and a ten-gallon hat labouring among rows of green shoots where the tilled soil of established fields was once more visible.

Feeling by instinct that the worker beyond him was the master of the property which he was approaching, Archer turned his horse off the dirt track that he had been following out of the east and slanted into the band of unploughed land between the two nearest of the fields on his left, halting his mount and swinging down as near to the stout labourer as he could get without actually treading on planted earth. 'Mr Luker?' he called tentatively.

The man in the field raised his head and craned. Then he turned his whole body and faced his visitor, dropping his hoe in the process and wiping his hands on the seat of his overalls. 'Who wants me?' he enquired.

'Bob Archer, Mr Luker. I'm Ray's brother.'

Luker shambled over to where Archer stood. He was a man whose height in no way matched his girth, and he had an unshaven face that was among the most crumpled and underhung that his caller had ever seen. 'Bob, eh?' the farmer said, offering a thick hand with spatulate fingers. 'Heard you was acomin'. Well met, then, and how are you?'

'Up to scratch, thank you,' Archer responded, 'and hope I see you the same. But this visit ain't what you might call a social one.'

'Oh? I'm Jack.'

'You know my name,' Archer said, smiling faintly as their hands parted. 'Ray's been shot.'

'Y'don't say,' Luker spat. 'Accident?'

'Anything but.'

The fat landsman's face tightened and lost what could only be described as its vacuousness. 'This don't sound good. Tell me what happened.'

Archer nodded and started telling him. He named Tug Filby, the Broken M's foreman, as the shooter, and went on to recount for Luker what had recently passed

49

between him and Anne Archer—though he toned what he had to say down in the most diplomatic of fashions, thus keeping most of the woman's eloquence and passion out of it; but even so Luker's blackish and fading eye was quick to narrow and his expression echoed a kind of distant understanding of what had occurred. 'That's about it, Jack,' Archer suddenly concluded. 'Maybe it wants a bit of sense, but there you are.'

'I'm mighty sorry about Ray,' Luker said. 'He's a friend and good neighbour—a man I'd do most anything for. Funny thing, Bob, but I recall hearin' a shot a while ago and didn't give it a thought. Y'know, when you get right down to your work, y'don't pay much mind to a lot else.' He sniffed hard, the noise suggesting stuffy sinuses. 'Son, you mustn't take offence at Missus Ray. She does have an edge to that tongue of hers, but she's a good sort. On what I've heard about you, you can't know her well. You haven't been around Ray's family much o' recent years, have you?'

'Of any years,' Archer confessed.

'That girl lost her father and two brothers in the war,' Luker explained. 'All three on the same day at Gettysburg. Ray told me—'cos Anne don't talk about it ever.'

'Heck of a blow,' Archer conceded. 'You have to feel a pang for her, Jack. I was part of the cavalry that got there too late. It's all history now.' He swore under his breath and scratched at an irritation on his belly that he didn't have. 'So what's your account of this water business? Except for my news concerning Ray, I can't have said much that you didn't know and were already fed up with.'

'Ain't that the solemn truth!' Luker declared. 'Bit of a facer, son, and what's happened today has made it all the worse. What are we to do with it?'

'Can it be that bad?'

'Sure can.'

'How so, Jack? You've got that agreement the late Shamus Manderson wrote out, haven't you?'

'I wish,' Luker said uncomfortably. 'And thereby, as that fellow Wister has it, hangs a tale.'

'No—you don't have it?'

'No—I don't have it. How much plainer do I have to be?'

Archer suppressed his rising temper. 'Where is it? You must know'

'I don't—not for sure,' Luker admitted. 'I can only think Mary Lewis took it when she left my house.'

'When she left your house? Where'd she go?'

'Ah, now,' Luker said. 'I can't go accusin'. Maybe she'll see what she's done and bring it back. Or send it.'

'Who is this Mary Lewis?' Archer demanded, slightly confused on the one hand and rather mystified on the other. 'I wish you'd say things plain.'

'She's a girl,' Luker said. 'Sort of

mixture of nurse and housemaid, as you might say, but not too much of either.'

The farmer went on to explain how his wife, Edie Luker, had become ill last year and he'd been forced to advertise for help in the house. The applicants for the work he'd offered were few, but the best suited of them had seemed to be Mary Lewis, a girl from Kansas who had been brought up in an orphanage and had no family. She had been mixing the duties of housemaid and carer for years—when not doing a turn as a nanny—and had supplied excellent references. The arrangement had proved a good one while Mrs Luker had been bedridden but, when she had begun to recover and wanted to regain control of running her home, the two women had clashed 'somethin' awful' and Jack Luker had soon been forced to tell Mary that he thought it would be better for all concerned if she looked for another position. This she had done—been almost immediately successful—and gone her way last week.

'Where?' Archer demanded, feeling that they had been a long way round to get back to this particular question mark.

'Well, that's just it,' Luker said, hedging again.

'Far?'

'No, just up the hill.'

'Up the hill?' Archer looked round sharply at the ridge to the north of them. 'Up there? Do you mean she went to the Manderson ranch?'

Luker jerked his chin mechanically. He looked both blank and glum.

'Great day!' Archer protested. 'If that water agreement went with her, it's little wonder my brother got shot. There's no longer any proof down here you farmers have the right to get your water from Cold Wells.'

'You can't be sure of that.'

'I've seen three-legged cows,' Archer responded sourly, 'but they don't come

54

along all that often. Use your head, mister!'

'Now, son, that ain't polite,' Luker said frostily, though the sternness in his voice didn't quite convince. 'You mind your manners if you want to go on talkin' to me. It won't help anything if we start spittin' at one another.'

Archer took a breath that was slow and deep, controlling himself again. 'All right. I was shooting off my mouth. There must be a copy or a record of your agreement with Shamus Manderson in town. I understand it was notarized.'

'It was. But all that was twenty years and more ago.'

'So what?'

'Things happen in course o' time.'

'What things?' Archer asked, closing both his eyes and his fists.

'Well—fires and such.'

'You trying to tell me all legal proof that agreement existed has been burned up?'

''Fraid so'

'When? How?'

'Last Christmas,' Luker replied. 'Lawyer Hughes's records went up in smoke. His premises would have burned down if the blaze hadn't been spotted in time. Too much firing jammed into the pot-bellied stove. So I was told.'

'How many coincidences do you want?' Archer inquired, beyond anger now and feeling little but helpless disgust. 'Jack, I'm sorry, but if you met the granddaddy of 'em all, I doubt you'd recognize it. And why didn't my sister-in-law tell me about the fire, I wonder?'

''Cos she didn't know, I expect.'

'Sounds like you've been keeping quiet about what you know.'

'Nope. Haven't seen anybody to discuss it with. Folk work hard in these parts and talk little.' Luker took another of his stuffy sniffs. 'We don't all spend our lives gallivantin' around the countryside and mindin' business that ain't our own.'

'Now you watch it, suh!' Archer advised grimly.

'It's all as it is, Bob, and there ain't a blamed thing I can alter.'

'I disagree, Mr Luker,' Archer said coldly. 'That agreement was in your keeping. It was your responsibility. Now it's gone, and it sounds to me as if only Mary Lewis could have taken it. She's a thief, and you should have gone after her long before this.'

Luker wagged a finger in his visitor's face. 'You listen to me, young fellow. The girl could have taken that piece of paper by mistake. It's possible she ain't aware of it even now.'

'I don't see how that could be so.'

'You will,' Luker insisted, 'you will.'

'Are you telling me you honestly believe there are such circumstances?'

'Haven't you lived long enough yet, boy,' Luker asked, now very much on his dignity, 'to have learned that things ain't always what they appear?'

'Very well,' Archer advised, feeling the knock back, 'put me right—though I figure it must have been you put me wrong in the first place.'

'It's all on account of an arrangement me and the missus have at home,' Luker explained, going on to tell Archer about the escritoire that stood at the back of his parlour and had a big middle drawer which was used to contain family documents and such correspondence as came the household's way. Luker informed his listener that Mary Lewis had had the complete freedom of the dwelling while she had worked for him and got into the habit of putting her letters—of which she had received quite a few, since several folk by whom she had earlier been employed remained her friends and kept in touch—in with the Luker correspondence and such. 'So,' the farmer ended, 'it's quite possible that when the girl removed her letters from the drawer before she left us, she picked up a handful of stuff that wasn't all her own. It's easily done in haste, Bob. You must allow that.'

'I suppose it could've happened like that,' Archer said, 'but you wouldn't convince me of it if you talked all day long. What's more, I don't believe you credit it either. You've been slack, and you're covering up for yourself.'

'That's offensive!'

'It sure is!'

Luker ground his teeth and shook a fist. 'If I was a few years younger—'

'You're not,' Archer cut in—'and you never saw the day; so you can stow that as fast as you like.'

'You're a nasty man, Bob Archer!'

'Dead right, mister,' his caller agreed; 'and I'm about to go down a whole lot further in your estimation. You're gutless. You haven't been up there after Mary Lewis because you're afraid of what might happen to you on the Broken M if you did. That's the truth, ain't it? You know how many beans make five, you old sooner!'

'You don't know pig's end from pork!' Luker yapped, spiteful in his turn. 'You'd accuse anybody of any damned thing, 'cos you're like that! But I can't—and won't—accuse a girl of being a thief without bein' sure.'

'I'm not quarrelling with that,' Archer returned flatly. 'But don't come over self-righteous with me when you've taken no step to discover what actually happened. You should have gone up to the Manderson ranch long before this—asked for Mary Lewis, taken her aside, and got the truth out of her.'

'Time—that's the bugbear! I haven't got the time. I'm the slave of this here farm!'

Archer ran a disdainful eye up and down Luker's fat body. 'What are you giving me?' he demanded. 'You don't strike me as a man who slogs his guts out all the hours that God sends. I'll swear you don't work any harder than you have to, and that you have hours to spare in every day. No, it's not lack of time. It's lack of courage!'

'God damn you!'

'This is a damned generation,' Archer sighed. 'You, me, the whole blasted lot of us!'

'You go up there!' Luker roared with the flinching defiance of a weak man who was trying to sound strong. 'Don't hide behind smart words! You've put your nose in, now let's see what you're made of?' Everything about the farmer—expression, gesture, and stamping foot—became provocative. 'Only you be careful, Sonny Jim! You ain't got a passel o' rough riders around you any more. You'll get your comb cut if you throw your weight about in these parts. We don't need no lynchin' vigilante to show us how!'

Archer tried to ignore that one. The words just spoken were words that he had not wished to hear—or even really expected to. There were folk around who suspected what he had been, but few had any real proof of it. Clearly, Luker knew what he knew and others locally must do the same. Words flew like iron filings to the magnet, and brothers and nephews talked—in pride or even sadness—and the result, no matter how long it took, was that people round and about came to a deeper understanding and knew too much. The Yankees would still hang him if they could lay hands on him, the Texas Rangers would throw him into jail as a matter of political expediency, and the local law would probably chase him out if the more important local citizens identified him and began to couple his name with words of hate—which meant that he would do well to avoid pushing those who had an inkling of his extra-judicial activities since the war too far. 'You want me to visit the Manderson ranch?' he said quietly. 'You've got your wish. I'll ride up to the Broken M right now and put the questions to Mary Lewis. Somebody has got to do it. I'm sure the girl has robbed and betrayed you, but we nevertheless have to make absolutely certain of it. If there's the smallest chance that the written agreement Shamus Manderson had with you farmers can be recovered, it must be taken.'

'I reckon.'

'If it's gone for good, are you landsmen ready to fight?'

'Gun trouble?'

'What else?'

'Don't talk it up,' Luker said emptily, staring at the ground. 'There must be some other way.'

'Folk say that,' Archer warned, 'but sometimes there isn't. If you lose your water, everything will go. For you and your families. There'll be no future. All those years of sweat and strain will stand for nothing. The Mandersons are the new face of the West. The cattle business is all that counts with them. Once let them get away with running some of you farmers off your land, Jack, and it will happen everywhere. There'll be no end to it.' Moving to his horse, he swung up and settled into leather. 'Have I spoken you false?'

'No,' Luker admitted, 'I don't think you have.'

'Then let's forget the squabbling, Jack,' Archer said deliberately. 'Ray expects to keep me around, and my cause can't stand it.'

'Ain't that a fact, boy!' Luker responded knowingly, and not without a note of triumph in his voice. 'Told you, I'd do most anything for Ray.'

'Sure,' Archer acknowledged. 'Understood. Now—what's the best way up to the Manderson place?'

'Well, that's an easy one anyhow,' the older man said. 'If you keep ridin' west for about quarter of a mile, you'll see the ranch path leadin' up through the ridge to the high grass. The path'll carry you straight on into Orv Manderson's yard. Two miles, or mebbe a bit more.'

'Thanks.'

'You be careful now.'

Archer grinned bleakly. It seemed to him that he had heard those words before. They were simple enough, yet covered so many meanings. In the present instance, it occurred to him that if he were that careful of himself he wouldn't have involved himself in any of this. It had never been his fight, and the family connection was not that important. He had fought his own battles without even the blessing of those of his own blood. Now here he was on the verge of entering danger at the spur of moral blackmail from a crafty old farmer. For a moment he was tempted to head west and keep going, regardless of the possessions which he had left at his brother's farm. His arrangements with Ray were in fact tentative, and he hadn't actually thrown in his lot with the man. Yet he had been behaving otherwise from the start. Why, hell—he could not even be sure that he had it in him to be a tiller of the soil! And hadn't he thought vaguely of beginning some business of his own? He could do that most any place. But he felt committed. The momentum of this affair had already picked him up. Given the necessary directions, he would have gone ahead without any prompting from Jack Luker. Free will? It was a treacherous notion at best. Conscience ruled, and blood was thicker than water. Especially a brother's blood. 'So long, Jack,' he said resignedly; then jerked his mount's head to the right and fetched the animal about, kneeing it back in the direction of the dirt path.

Was he a quarter of a mile from that ranch trail—or eternity? Better go and find out.

FOUR

Archer rode along distractedly. His mind was still disturbed by his recent quarrelling and troubled thoughts. He had always known that Texas was big, but today it stretched and stretched before him, and the sky was a mighty arch above him that went on and on just like the land. The two seemed to meet outside measurable distance—where the hazes of illusion shaped new worlds—and the stillness was as total near and far as that in the gleaming fields of the midheaven. For all the brightness there was a loneliness present too—one with which Archer was all too familiar—yet he had never fully experienced it before this while in his own company, and the sensation seemed to have a draining effect on his body and mind. Even his spirit. There was a knowledge of change present too, and it was years since he had last felt anything like it. He'd have been far more confident about what he was doing now if he had still had the Sadd River Vigilantes at his back, but they were disbanded and long gone. Perhaps a man only found out how much of a man he really was when he had to depend entirely on himself. Like this.

He saw on his right the track of which Jack Luker had told him. Broad and deeply worn by waggon wheels and iron-shod hooves, it curved upwards across a slope of coarse grass—moving slightly to the east of northpoint—and he could make out where it broke through the underlying sandstone of the ridge it breached and appeared to draw a final line beneath the sky; which was another of those illusions, for the impressions in the earth down here confirmed the abundance of life on the high plains beyond. There, then, was his path, and he turned his horse on to the ranch trail and let it make its own pace upwards.

The grassy slope was not without its rock-piles. These threw up heaps of debris at irregular intervals on either hand. Not that Archer had the least interest in them, and might have reached the top of his climb almost unaware of their presence, but he was in fact no more than half way up the incline, when a voice bawled at him, from the top of a pile on his right and perhaps two hundred yards ahead, in tones that were about as challenging and belligerent as they could get. 'Turn back! You're ridin' on private property! Trespassers ain't allowed on this ranch!'

Archer was incensed and drew up straight in his saddle. 'How about visitors?'

'Them neither!'

Judging that the man atop the boulders was the one who had earlier begun shadowing him along the summit of the ridge from a point close to where his brother's ranch was situated, Archer shouted: 'You go to hell!'

'That's where you'll be going if you ain't careful!'

'Not if you can't handle your gun better than you shoot off that mouth of yours!'

'I can shoot, Bobby—and well you know it!'

Archer was a trifle daunted now, and tempted to draw rein, but he went on jogging to the front all the same. 'Is that Dan Burton?'

'It is.'

'I thought your boss might have let a braying donkey out for a turn on the grass!'

'You keep a civil tongue in your head, Archer!' Burton cautioned. 'Don't go lookin' for any favours from me on account of the past!'

This was a fine turn up and no mistake! Archer pulled a face over this latest piece of bad luck. He had lately imagined all his old comrades hundreds of miles away by now, but it seemed that one of them—by chance

70

or even design—had found a gun job with the Mandersons. If such a thing had had to happen, any one of the Sadd River boys would have been preferable to Dan Burton. Burton had been the one fellow with whom he couldn't get on. The man was big, bullying, ill-tempered, lazy and selfish—a thoroughgoing son-of-a-bitch who had run the entire gamut of crime and brutality and was nobody's friend. Just when Archer could have done with a pal showing up, it seemed that the devil had sent Burton along to be his enemy. But he must not show fear. Dan Burton would snap at that like a hungry dog at red meat. He must keep riding forward, and try to make his erstwhile comrade back down. For he could not believe that—in the present circumstances—Burton would risk gunning down an unarmed man in cold blood. It was most unlikely that he had been given orders to that effect, and was probably following his own thuggish inclinations at the moment. 'I'm coming up!' Archer called in a voice that was as leisurely as he could make it. 'I've got to see Mr Orville Manderson, and have a few words with Miss Mary Lewis. Matter of some urgency!'

'Go back, Bobby!' Burton insisted, the threat in his tones undoubtedly real.

Archer kept the rowels gently prodding at his mount's flanks. It was not his intention to give an inch—even if it meant getting knocked ass-over-tip by a slug.

'You reckless bastard!' Burton roared. 'On your own head be it!'

Winchester drawn into his right shoulder, Burton rose up atop his rockpile. Flinching despite himself, Archer watched the man linger for a moment over his aim; then he saw the rifle flash and heard it roar, the bullet burying itself in the trail below his mount's jaw. The impact caused the horse to back up and rear, forelegs cycling, and Archer yanked the animal's head to the left and leaned forward in his stirrups, finding the exact balance he needed and setting the mount down on the trailside. He was aware of his skill, but made his deftness appear a casual thing. Then squaring his horse to the climb again, he resumed moving to the front and upwards, knowing that his action amounted to an outright provocation which was even more gross than before.

Burton swore at the top of his voice, his fury an almost tangible force. Now his rifle pumped out fire and smoke, and its echoes pulsed back off the ridge and went cracking and rolling southwards like young thunder. Bullets laced the air around the rider's seated figure. Archer heard his cantle splinter, and smelled scorching hair as hot lead whipped his horse's mane. It was all pretty unnerving, and Archer had to grit his teeth and gaze skywards as he strove to maintain a relentless progress that seemed to ignore the presence of the gun.

Archer had never doubted Burton's ability as a marksman. The fellow was one of the very best shots that he had ever met, and he was relying on the other's eye as much as anything else in his maddening exploitation of Burton's anger and indignation; but the man's skills were not perfect and the bark of his Winchester seemed to grow more and more excited, until he shot too close and ripped a long white streak across the offside flank of Archer's horse that all but instantly filled with blood. Then, shrilling its agony, the mount seemed to rocket almost to the vertical—shooting its rider out of his hull and backwards to the ground—and, while Archer lay there with his brain spinning, began chasing itself in rapid circles and biting at its wound like a beast of the wild.

The Winchester fell silent and, as the moments went by, the semi-crazed activity of the horse reduced by degrees until its circling petered out and it came to a stop, facing in the wrong direction and snorting and blowing to itself as it now began jerking its head up and down and producing a small music from its bit-chain. Getting a grip on his balance, Archer thrust himself to his feet and stood gazing dizzily towards the marksman atop the rock-pile from which the recent hail of bullets had flown. He watched Burton's hulking shape as the rifleman bent into priming his weapon's magazine with a handful of cartridges taken from a trouser-pocket, and wondered what to look for next if he braced the other again; but he was spared the need of finding out when the sound of a woman's voice reached him suddenly in a peremptory shout from higher up the grade and Archer lifted his eyes to see a female rider—who was beautifully turned out in a blue silk shirt, flat-crowned taupe plains hat, and figured riding leathers—galloping downhill towards him and Burton on a palomino mare that looked worth more money than Archer had ever handled at one time during his whole life.

As Archer began to brush himself down in an absent manner, the approaching

75

girl checked her golden horse opposite the rock-pile on which Dan Burton was poised and shouted upwards: 'Get out of here, you numbskull! Take yourself back where you came from! Who told you to begin shooting up visitors to the Broken M?'

'Ain't like that, Miss Kathleen!' Burton yelped in protest. 'That fellow is—'

'I can't stand the sight of you!' the girl declared, nudging her horse back into motion.

'Yes, Miss Manderson,' Burton responded, frowning dismally and touching his hat. Then, with surprising speed for so big a man, he vanished down the back of the boulder-heap and must have climbed to the ground very quickly indeed, for he reappeared only moments later—mounted now—and sent his horse galloping up the land behind the pile of sandstone debris, heading for the break in the ridge above through which the ranch track passed, and all before Kathleen Manderson had reached Archer's position and stopped at his side.

The girl knocked back her hat and, smiling with great charm, bent forward a little and said: 'I apologise for that man. It seems we lost most of the help worthy of hiring to the war.'

'Reckon you're right about that,' Archer acknowledged. 'Don't you worry none about Dan Burton and his ways. That guy's too stupid to button his trousers.'

'You obviously know him,' the girl said dryly. 'Are you all right? That was quite a tumble you took!'

'You saw it?' Archer said inconsequentially. 'Yeah, I'll do. The name's Archer—Bob Archer. I'm Ray's brother. Yonder at the farm. If you know him?'

'Yes, I know him. Anne too. They're a good couple; salt of the earth.'

'You're Miss Manderson, eh?'

'Kathleen, yes—Orville's daughter.' The delicately tinted oval of the face under her quiffed up blonde hair showed a quick sensibility. 'You look surprised.'

'Hadn't heard you mentioned,' he answered frankly, 'that's all.'

'It's a man's world on the high grass,' the girl said dismissively, yet not without a hint of bitterness. 'I'm a year older than my brother Jem, but I don't figure.'

'That I can't believe,' Archer said, even franker than before and no less admiring. 'You'd figure anywhere.'

'How's that?'

'You're the most beautiful woman I ever saw. With looks like yours, Miss Kathleen, you could conquer the world. Cleopatra didn't do so badly, did she?'

'A girl of a darker hue, I think.'

'Who cares about hues?'

'Not you, I'm sure,' Kathleen Manderson confided, laughter dancing in the blue of her candid stare. 'It may be that you hadn't heard of me, Bob Archer, but I've heard you spoken of. Often.'

'I wish it had been different,' Archer replied wryly. 'I was never among the country's best beloved.'

'I was never struck on mutual admiration, were you?'

'No, Miss Manderson,' he returned, stressing her title.

'Well, Mr Archer,' she said, changing tack and becoming distinctly businesslike, 'what are you here for?'

'I guess I've a bone to pick with your father,' Archer admitted; 'but that's too serious to risk quarrelling with you about. I want a word with Mary Lewis also.'

'You're unarmed,' Kathleen Manderson observed. 'That's a good sign.'

He suspected the girl of irony—for she, like others around here, appeared to know more than he liked concerning his reputation and bloody works—and was tempted to inform her that virtue hadn't entered into it and that he had merely forgotten to buckle on his gunbelt before coming out, but he liked the seemingly good opinion that she had held of him up to now and wanted to hang on to it for as long as he could. 'Is it all right,' he asked, 'if I climb back on my horse and pick up riding my errand again where I left off?'

'Surely.'

'Thank you,' he said, rounding the rear end of his horse and inspecting the wound left where the bullet had ploughed along its flank. The damage was still bloody, but not too deep and, after patting the beast and assuring it that it would live, he ducked round the mount's head and gathered his dangling reins, swinging up a moment later. 'Goodbye then.'

'No,' the girl said, 'I'm coming with you.'

'Up to you,' Archer replied. 'I thank you for telling Dan Burton where to get off.'

Kathleen Manderson wheeled her palomino about, and they set off up the top third of the climb, their mounts moving at a slow trot. There was silence between them until after they had passed through the break in the ridge and begun crossing the plain beyond it. Then the girl asked:

'What is your difference with my father?' And, when he didn't reply and had had plenty of extra time to do so, added: 'I'd better warn you, Mr Archer, I'm persistent. You might as well tell me what I want to know first as last.'

'I don't want you to cut up rough.'

'I'm not going to.'

'You can't be sure of that.'

'In this case I think I can,' she said. 'You've behaved very well. I'm the one who's behaving badly.'

The girl was fair enough, Archer liked that, and even believed what she had said. 'All right. Tug Filby, your foreman, I believe, put a slug in my brother's shoulder an hour or two ago. It happened when Ray and Harry, my nephew, were at Cold Wells to fill their water barrel. Your people had no acceptable right to be corralling that water, but I figure what happened was all part of your pa's determination to drive the farmers down there off their land. You know about that, don't you?'

'Yes,' Kathleen Manderson admitted heavily.

'Do you think it's right?'

'No.'

'But?'

'He's my father. The wells belonged to my late grandfather to begin with. And our ranch is now expanding at a rate where our stock needs that water.'

'Fiddlesticks!' Archer scoffed. 'As I understand that Peter Blood business, the land south of the wells was all his and dependent on that water. Your grandfather gave up his right to the wells in exchange for the right to graze his cattle on more than a thousand acres of grass—and that's a heap of land, y'know—out to the east of my brother's place. Your cows have no more ease of access to Cold Wells right now than they had when your grandpa and Peter Blood sat down to draw up their paper. The only way that water will achieve real value is if the grass below the ridge behind us is all in your pa's hands and he can run his cattle on it as he likes. Case proved against your father. Even a simple guy like myself can see that.'

'There never was much point arguing with the obvious,' Kathleen Manderson said in response, sighing heavily. 'You want to show my dad in the worst light. He's a tough man—and he wants what he wants, like his own father before him—but he's also fair. If the farmers would only show a willingness to negotiate, he'd talk turkey and buy them out top dollar; but he knows that's too much to hope for. Jack Luker won't budge a clod, your brother is the same, and the rest of them are no better. Everything is against my father. It drives the poor man to desperation!'

'It appears to me he's got land enough,' Archer returned bluntly. 'Your pa reminds me of the fat guy who wants to stuff himself until he busts. How much do you Mandersons want? Look at yourself, dammit! You've got all there is. You can only eat so much, drink so much, live under one roof at a time, and enjoy the freedom to go where you like and do what you like within the law. Beyond that, life becomes kinda pointless, y'know. The squirrel that piles up too many nuts to see it through the winter only sees what it can't use go rotten. All nature is somewhat the same, Miss Manderson. Your father seems to me big enough all ready. He's a real successful guy!'

'It's his philosophy that a business can never get too big,' the girl explained. 'The thing that doesn't grow, Mr Archer, starts to die. Isn't that also true throughout nature?'

'Just maybe,' Archer conceded. 'And it's Bob if we're goin' on like this. Mr Archer was my old man; he's dead, long since. But it all depends on what you mean by growth. Folk and their lives can grow in all manner of ways. I know I'm just a simple—'

'You're far from a simple man,' Kathleen Manderson interrupted. 'I'll grant you're uneducated, but that doesn't make you ignorant—and I can see for myself that you lack sophistication, but that doesn't make you crude. You're bright as a new pin, and your character is solid. I trust you. If it hadn't been so, you wouldn't have got this far, and I would not be riding beside you at this moment.'

'Well, bully for you, Miss Manderson!' Archer applauded ironically. 'Thanks for telling me about myself. I hadn't the first idea. I do declare!'

'If we're going to have a row after all,' the blonde said severely, pulling her still cuffed-back hat squarely onto her crown, 'you might as well shorten up the broadsides by calling me Kathleen or Kathy. Dad and my brother always call me Kathy. Mother always called me "Irish". But, like your father, she's dead and gone.'

'My mother too,' Archer said; 'even before the old man. So—if there's an inner circle I'm joining it. Look here, Kathy.

What your pa appears to be threatening is criminal. It could get him jailed—or even hung. When him and me stand face to face, I won't be able to say less.'

'I'm not sure he's threatening anything,' the girl mused. 'His talk indoors is sometimes unwise, but whose isn't if we get riled up? You tell me your brother has been shot. I'd want to hear all sides of it before I blamed Tug Filby for what happened. Ray's a touchy customer. As for Tug, he's right up to the mark. He wouldn't be our foreman if he wasn't. Bob, you've handled men and know what it's all about. If Filby wasn't prepared to live and die for us, he wouldn't be worth the salary we pay him.'

Archer saw some flowers growing in the slightly damp earth beneath the horn end of a canted anvil of stone. 'Even Solomon in all his glory,' he said enigmatically, 'was not arrayed such as these.'

But the girl picked up his meaning instantly. 'My dad doesn't regard himself as the wiseman of the prairies, you know. He isn't a crook either. I told you how the farmers drive him to desperation. They do still have the contract that Peter Blood drew up with my grandfather. Jack Luker holds it for them all.'

'Wrong,' Archer said flatly. 'He ain't holding it for anybody right now. It's flown beyond his ken. I'm betting it took wing when Mary Lewis left his house. What d'you suppose I want to speak with that woman for?'

Kathleen Manderson appeared momentarily shocked, amazed—and even frightened. 'What are you feeding me?'

'It ain't birdseed,' Archer assured her. 'It used to be called the truth, and it can be mighty indigestible stuff.'

'The truth!' she exclaimed, tossing her head, though her expression suggested that she knew more than he and that her knowledge was worrying her. 'How do you know all this? How are you able to tell me?'

He gave her a rough and heavily edited account of the visit he had earlier paid Jack Luker and of what had passed between them. He was also forced, by the girl's perceptive promptings, into repeating a little of the angry exchanges between Anne Archer, his sister-in-law, and himself, and Kathleen Manderson was intuitive enough to end up demanding: 'Why couldn't you listen to Anne? The best way of avoiding trouble is not to make it. But, no! Our hero has to set it all to rights!'

'Somebody had to come up here,' Archer informed her. 'It ought to have been Jack Luker, but he hasn't got the guts of a louse! If you were as surprised as you seemed to be when I spoke of Mary Lewis and what I deem her theft a short while ago, maybe you'll help me to convince the woman that she should repent of what she's done and return the Cold Wells water agreement to its rightful owners—not pass it on to somebody who'll destroy it and perhaps her too.'

'Do you know what you're saying?' Kathleen Manderson asked in tones that were almost anguished. 'You should just hear yourself! I'm fast losing patience with you. Haven't you a kindly thought for my family at all? Have you no respect for us?'

'It's not a matter of what I feel or don't feel,' Archer replied, trying to be totally objective, while taking in the wide spread of ranch buildings which was now rising out of the land before them and dominated by a house of true size and some architectural magnificence, if the eye could stand the neo-Gothic lines of the day. 'Heck, Kathy, every word I've spoken has come out of the evidence already present—no part of which I've had any hand in putting there.'

'Then what I've still to tell you won't help.'

'What's that?'

'I don't want to tell you,' the blonde said, her reluctance almost choking her.

'I wouldn't, but I don't see how you can miss finding out.'

He waited for it.

'Mary and my brother Jem are courting. They're about to get engaged.'

'I need no more proof of anything,' Archer observed sadly. 'That satisfies me. The girl will already have put victory into your father's hands. I see it as her way into your family. Why didn't Jack Luker mention this love affair between Mary Lewis and your brother?'

'It follows he didn't know about it,' Kathleen Manderson answered. 'I expect she kept her dalliance quiet—for obvious reasons.'

'Happen you're right,' Archer conceded. 'I reckon Jack would have been livid if he'd known what Miss Mary was up to in her spare time.' Out of deference to his companion, he resisted the impulse to spit and added: 'I seem to have lost whatever reason I ever had for riding up here. In fact I can't honestly see myself as having a real place in what's been happening any longer. I don't know what can be done about that blamed agreement in the circumstances that appear to exist now.'

'Are you going to turn back, Bob?'

Archer felt baffled; his lines of thought and vision had become tangled and confused. 'I simply don't know what to do. The next move seems to lie with your papa.

'You—you could have a talk with my father.'

'And discuss what?' Archer sighed. 'Orville Manderson appears to hold all the cards that matter. There's only war left for the farmers, and that's the one certainty.'

'I won't hear talk of fighting, Bob!' the blonde protested. 'At worst my father will invoke the law.'

'And what kind of cock-and-bull yarn will he tell the sheriff?'

'I believe you meant that as a rhetorical question, Bob.'

'Rheta—what-the-hell!' Archer snarled,

yanking his mount's head to the right in a moment of supreme frustration and intending to return to the ridge, now the better part of two miles to their rear, at full gallop; but his purpose was instantly obstructed in the most physical of manners as a party of riders came surging out of a nearby fold in the land before him and began closing upon him and his companion at speed. The horsemen were led by a middle-aged man of an obviously superior type who sat tall upon his black stallion and was dressed in a light-coloured corduroy jacket and riding britches, wore knee-length boots that shone like glass, and had upon his head a dove grey Stetson. To this masterful character's right rode Dan Burton, and to his left a powerful, dark-eyed man, with the healthiest of aquiline faces that was decorated by black sideburns and a thin moustache, while his appearance of strength and toughness was further emphasized by a variety of battle scars around the eyes that could only have been picked up in the course of numerous fist-fights. The fellow also carried a bone-handled Colt in a position that suggested he was an expert in its use and, judging by the cleanliness of his range garb and air of authority, Archer put him down for Tug Filby, the Broken M's foreman.

So here would seem to be the owner of the ranch, his ramrod, and the trouble-maker of the moment. But beyond that, every man present was clearly hand-picked and to attempt running away from them would be futile; so it appeared that Archer was going to have a talk with Orville Manderson whether he liked it or not.

FIVE

Bringing his horse to a stop, Archer drew breath and sat waiting, the air finally bursting from his lungs as a sigh of both resignation and resolve as the ranch party halted a few yards beyond him and the man dressed in the light-coloured corduroy garments glanced quickly round at Dan Burton and asked: 'Is that Bob Archer?'

'Yes, Mr Manderson,' Burton replied fawningly. 'He's bad medicine, sir.'

'Are you bad medicine, Archer?' Manderson inquired, chin dipped and lower lip thrusting upwards to increase the sternness of his steely-eyed gaze.

'Only when others don't like my bottle,' Archer responded.

'Should I like it?'

'Doubt not.'

95

'Then it sounds to me like you're a fool to have come here, Archer. We don't suffer fools gladly.'

'Dad,' Kathleen Manderson began pleading, 'he's not looking for—'

'You keep out of this, Kathy!' her father ordered peremptorily, cutting her off with a gesture that was little short of a blow in itself. 'Never interfere between men!'

'She's been a lady to me, Mr Manderson,' Archer said, holding the other's eye and causing the rancher to blink, 'and a credit to you. Don't go and spoil it.'

'Don't you speak up to the boss like that!' the man with the aquiline face and all the scars warned sharply.

'He ain't my boss,' Archer reminded. 'Filby?'

'I'm Tug Filby, yes.'

'Then you and me have a bone to pick, mister,' Archer said grimly. 'You put a slug in my brother Ray, and he came home hurting bad.'

'He asked for it!' Filby declared. 'I told

him the boss had put the water in Cold Wells off limits to the farmers, but he refused to listen. He tried to use his rifle on me, but I put a stop to that.'

'You had no right to say the water was off limits,' Archer retorted, 'and Mr Manderson had no right to tell you it was.'

'Hear that, sir?' Filby asked in tones of outrage.

'I heard it, Tug,' the rancher said shortly. 'I have a map which proves beyond all question that Cold Wells were part of the land my father claimed back in the Eighteen-forties.'

'Wouldn't question it,' Archer replied flatly. 'But your pa and a guy named Peter Blood put their maps together and did some dickering. As a result of that, you got a big piece of the low land east of here to use as graze and Blood got the right to draw water from Cold Wells. They had a written agreement—duly notarized and standing at law—which covered their deal.

The contract, so far as I'm aware, runs in perpetuity and applies as surely today as it did twenty years ago. That means Tug Filby—and you as his employer, Mr Manderson—committed a crime against my brother this day for which he has every right to take you to court.'

'Shut up, you dog-eared ne'er-do-well!' the rancher commanded, rising up in his stirrups and glowering down at his caller from the extra height he thus acquired. 'You yap like a third rate shyster yourself!' He sat down again, the slowness of this action causing his saddle to creak and its strings to ping. 'Now hear this. No such water agreement exists. Cold Wells are part of the Broken M—mine—and I have the documentation to prove it, where and when you like.'

'Thanks to Mary Lewis,' Archer acknowledged stonily. 'Well, stealing that contract from Jack Luker won't do her any good in the end; and, big as you think you are, you'll come out of it with the short end too. I've seen it too often to doubt.'

'Seen it—and done it,' Dan Burton said evilly, smirking.

'Dan,' Archer cautioned seriously, for the harm that his erstwhile follower had just insinuated could ultimately hurt him too, 'you may feel comfortable with these folk right now, but they'll only protect your hide for as long as it suits them. Savvy?'

'He has no need to,' Orville Manderson advised. 'You'd do well to keep your tongue off Mary Lewis. If you put about wicked stories concerning her, I'll make you pay.'

'Where and when you like,' Archer reminded. 'Any time.'

'It's as well for you,' Tug Filby gritted out, 'you had the sense come up here unarmed. If you'd come heeled, you'd have gone home on a buckboard with your middle shot out!'

'We can try that one too,' Archer returned easily enough. 'I hope you're better with a gun than you are your fists.

Your face tells its own story about that.'

'You don't dare!' Filby howled in disbelief. 'Do you know who you're talking to? I was the bareknuckle champion of the West Coast for several years—*the* Tug Filby, and I licked many a guy twice your size and ten times your force!'

'When they were liquored up, I expect,' Archer commented, raising his eyebrows inquiringly at Manderson. 'With your permission?'

'You don't have it!' the cattleman rapped out. 'Damn your cheek!'

'Without it then,' Archer said, completing his mount's turn into the south and stirring it with his knees.

'You stay where you are!' Manderson raged.

Archer took not a mite of notice. He walked his horse across the noses of those bearing the men who opposed him, touching his hat to Kathleen Manderson, who had pulled well clear of the doings and was now looking on with the kind of disapproving blankness which admitted her inability to influence what was happening in the smallest degree.

'Filby!' the rancher barked.

'Yes, sir,' his foreman responded, too ready by half; and the ground rang as the Broken M's ramrod sprang down from his saddle and headed for the slowly departing rider with hands crooked and reaching.

Archer gathered himself, watching Filby's approach from the corner of his left eye. He regarded the imminent conflict as having been inevitable, and had no intention of letting the other hammer him without putting up the kind of fight that all present would ever remember. So, with the decision made to do battle, his chief desire was to seize the initiative by the best means he could, and that meant making a surprise move which would exclude fairness and include striking the first blow—reprehensible in some eyes, perhaps, but always effective.

Stopping his horse abruptly, Archer lifted

the animal high and turned it at Filby, causing its whirling forelegs to knock him to the ground and hopefully damage him plenty; but in fact the foreman had had time to throw up his arms and protect his head, thus sustaining no more than the odd bruise and a bump which plainly jarred him breathless. As Archer sprang down from his horse—shoving at the beast and slapping it aside—Filby scrambled up almost straightaway, lunging at his attacker with fists clenched and eyes staring. Archer met the ex-prizefighter head to head, conscious that Filby would have been much wiser to have gone into retreat until he was fully recovered from his fall, but the foreman's mistake was potentially his gain and he set about taking full advantage of the situation that he had engineered, whacking over a left to Filby's right temple that burst open some of his opponent's old scars and sent blood streaming down his face.

Filby tried to cover up, a skilled pugilist

all right, but his timing was off and he left his elbows far enough apart for Archer to step in close and rifle a blow to the solar plexus that landed with unbroken force. Cheeks ashen and bile spilling from his lips, Filby dropped to his knees, and that ought to have been the signal for Archer to step back and give him a chance to regain his feet. But there was to be none of that. The only rule in this kind of fight was to win at all costs. So Archer brought up his right knee under the foreman's jaw and sent him crashing over backwards with his mouth a scarlet ruin out of which teeth flew.

The injured man lay spreadeagled and gasping. His eyes were closed and he was no better than semi-conscious. On any other occasion it would have been enough, but Archer meant to make a job of this one—since Tug Filby was the kind of adversary that a lucky victor should make sure that he never had to fight again—and he ran at his downed enemy, intending to drop knees-first onto the foreman's chest and crush his ribs and lungs, but he had yet to reach the other when a surging horse caught him from the left-hand side and sent him flying.

Archer went sprawling over the legs of his opponent. He lay with his nose to the ground, and had a brief mental vision of having been knocked off his feet by Orville Manderson's horse. He supposed that the rancher, feeling a responsibility for his foreman and recognizing that Archer was on the brink of doing Filby what could prove irreparable harm, had seen the need to intrude his presence and give his employee the chance to recover sufficiently to resume the fight, but he soon discovered his mistake. For, within moments of his own prostration, a heavy form crashed down upon his back and tried to pin him to the earth, while a fist thudded against the upper right-hand part of his neck and the side of his jaw.

This hurt more than stunned and,

enraged anew, Archer bent his spine and flung his attacker off him. Then, tipping over on to his backside and propping himself up with his hands, he spat blood and blinked narrowly, identifying the guy whom he had just pitched aside as Dan Burton. Burton had just reached the end of a rolling movement and come to rest several yards beyond the man whom he had tried to jump. He was stretched out on his right side and looking slightly dazed, and Archer reckoned that licking the tar out of the big guy would present no problem. In fact it was going to be a pleasure!

Archer began to rise, the muscles cording in his shoulders and arms, and he was almost ready to dive in at Burton, when he was once more surprised by the arrival of an attacker from behind and flattened again, this time with force enough to knock most of the wind out of him. After that two more assailants fell upon him from the rear, and it came to him, with a chilling sensation at the pit of his stomach, that he was no longer in a fight so much as a projected beating up. Panic filled him, and all the energy that his body still contained gathered itself at his heart and then detonated. Up he rose like an irresistible force, hurling his attackers from him and renewing his battle stance.

A face swam before Archer's eyes. He hit out as hard as he could, and the visage sank from view; but another appeared in the same instant and he struck at it, too, feeling blood splash into his face as this vanished also. After that figures surged at him thick and fast and, though Archer tried to punch them all, blows rained in upon him from all directions and his defence was quickly overwhelmed. Now blow after blow bounced off his temples, cheeks and jaw, and the sky rocked crazily in his vision and blood-flecked darkness blotted out his sight. Indeed, consciousness itself only remained with him because he was being punched so often by so many men that none of his attackers was given the chance to actually aim and deliver a knock-out blow—with the result that Archer was battered and far more hurt in the general sense than he would have been by a single measured punch that laid him low.

Archer staggered around under the battering for perhaps half a minute; then a scything boot swept the legs from under him and down he went. Now his enemies started to kick him, toes probing the soft tissues of his body for the points of greatest weakness, and there was no doubt that somebody's kick would soon have crippled him, when a rifle banged in the air and the attack on him ceased instantly. He was left lying prone and barely able to stir.

'Bob!' he heard Kathleen Manderson call to him anxiously. 'Are you all right?'

Willing himself to the effort, he turned over and sat up, his vision returning and every square inch of his body instantly filling with pain. 'Sure,' he choked out. 'I guess I'm still in one piece.'

'No thanks to my father and his men!' the girl declared scathingly.

Archer saw that she was holding a Winchester in her hands. He supposed that the rifle had been holstered on her mount all along, though he hadn't noticed it. The weapon was now cocked and covering the members of the ranch party—those still mounted and the others afoot—and the girl's expression was such that Archer had no doubt that she would fire on any man who made another offensive movement against him. 'They're a vicious pack of hounds, Kathy!' he rubbered out. 'Get your cook to throw 'em bones first thing!'

'They're savages!' the blonde agreed. 'But cowards first, and that's the worst of it. I'm ashamed of them, Bob—and my father most of all. He encouraged it! How could you, dad? How could you encourage eight men to set about one? I believe you'd have let them kill him!'

'He needs killing, my girl!' her father

retorted, using a note of parental authority to excuse the air of shamed defiance that he otherwise carried. 'He's an outlaw in all that matters. He—he challenged me! If there had been a tree handy, I'd have had him lynched.'

'How else could the man respond?' Kathy Manderson demanded contemptuously. 'He and the farmers on the Blood land have been wronged. Even terribly wronged! I don't know if grandfather can see us from where he is now; but, if he can, he must be weeping for what his son's done here. Power and money have gone utterly to your head!'

'Old as you are, Kathy,' her father warned, wagging a finger at her sternly, 'I'll tan your backside for you when you get home!'

'You'll ever regret it if you try it,' the girl warned.

'Try it,' Archer added, rising splay-footed and fixing the rancher with eyes that glittered through bruised slits, 'and before God, Satan, and all things good and evil, I swear I'll kill you!'

'You—you wouldn't d-dare!' Manderson spluttered, but the force of the warning had robbed his cheeks of their colour nevertheless.

'Try me,' Archer champed. 'Make my—'

'Can you ride, Bob?' Kathy interrupted.

'Near enough, I reckon.'

'Then get on your horse and let's hear no more about it!' the girl ordered. 'We poor women spend our best years bringing little boys up to lead decent lives, but you shame us at every turn when you become men!'

'Now you're going to let into me, I suppose,' Archer said grumpily, spitting out a tooth.

'I'm going to see you home.'

'I can get there by myself.'

'No, you can't.'

Archer went shambling towards his horse, blowing from first one side of his swelling head and then the other.

His experience of women had not been great—for his life had been too busy for much of that nonsense—but he knew instinctively that when a woman spoke as Kathleen Manderson had just spoken, a man had either to shut up or be foolishly brave. Well, he'd been brave enough for one day, and he doubted whether his body could stand any more foolishness, so he held his noise—except to swear softly under his breath—and climbed astride his mount like an old, old man. There he collapsed on the animal's neck, frankly incapable of reaching for his reins and glad just to hang on. It seemed that he did need a mite of care. Okay, let the girl help him. It might be as well if she kept out of her father's way for the time being. 'You coming then?' he enquired from the right-hand corner of his busted up mouth.

With her rifle tucked under her arm now and its muzzle pointing ever more acutely at her father and his men as she kneed her palomino out in front of Archer's horse and gathered up its reins, Kathleen Manderson halted again for just long enough to say: 'Go about your business, dad, and leave us to ours. If you send anybody after us, I'll shoot them. Is that plain enough for you?'

'All this over that piece of scum!' her father sneered at her. 'You always have had a weakness for undeserving cases, Kathy. What a man to take under your wing! I'd rather you'd gone off with a bad Yankee!' At that he made a sign to the members of his party still in their saddles and off they rode towards the not far distant ranch site, leaving those still afoot to sort themselves out and carry Tug Filby—who was still incapable of doing much for himself—to his horse and boost him into his hull, while the sagging Archer squinted back at the scene, as the blonde moved off with him in tow, and hated the foreman and his helpers with every fibre of his being.

Archer wasn't too sure of exactly what happened to him directly after that. He realized that Kathy Manderson was leading him eastwards rather than to the west, but the throbbing in his brain corresponded with long moments that he spent passing in and out of consciousness and the miles went by in a rather hazy and nightmarish fashion. He was also left with little awareness of the hour, and the sun seemed to have travelled much further across the sky by the time that his mind cleared completely and he was able to pick up his aching head and bring his normal intelligence to examining the land around him. What he saw was falling grass—a scene familiar to him and yet not instantly identifiable from his present angle of traverse—and he was forced to think about it before he grasped that his helper was guiding him home over the landbridge by which the Broken M cattle moved back and forth from the high graze to the low grass at the eastern end of the Blood country. It had indeed been the shorter and easier route from where they had started, and he could already see his brother's farm quite plainly across the downward tilt of the pastures to the right of him.

Sitting up straight and drawing a few deep breaths, Archer gingerly flexed his body and reckoned himself capable now of completing the ride under his own hand—and he had thoughts of telling Kathleen Manderson so—but there was something about the set of her head and shoulders from the rear view which discouraged him from this, and he decided that he would let the girl complete the task that she had given herself and find whatever satisfaction she could from the charity of her action. After all, he had needed her badly enough earlier—and there was a small voice within him that said he would be glad to go on needing her for as long as he had left to him—so perhaps his best 'thank you' and even his hope for the future would be in keeping a grateful silence now and allowing her to do the talking when they reached his brother's door.

The horses plodded steadily to the front, and the breeze met them out of the silence of the south and swirled and whispered onwards into the hush at their backs. There was a little peace in all this emptiness, with cows at one edge of it and the dark line where the earth met the sky taking in the rest. Archer relaxed inwardly, for it was the first time in hours that he hadn't felt threatened. Then Kathleen Manderson turned them both into the west, and they left the landbridge over a gentle descent towards ploughed soil.

This was the last half a mile. Now they approached Ray Archer's farm and, after a minute or so, young Harry, Bob's nephew, emerged from the front door of the house and stood watching them from the veranda. Soon the youngster craned, plainly calling to somebody indoors, and presently his mother came out and stood beside him, gazing eastwards no less intently than her son. 'Harry and Anne have come out to welcome you back,' blonde Kathy remarked, without turning her head, for the words were proof enough that she had known he was fully with her again and had perhaps been aware of it all along.

'I don't see the flags out,' Archer growled back uneasily, for he suddenly felt threatened again.

'Didn't I tell you?' Kathy said brightly. 'Anne and I get along fine.'

'Figures,' Archer muttered.

No more was said. The rest of the ground intervening was quickly covered. They entered the farmyard, and there Kathleen Manderson drew rein and Archer stopped his mount at a word. Now Anne Archer descended the veranda steps and walked out across the chicken-limed ground to meet them. She smiled first at the blonde, then uttered a loud sigh and frowned at her brother-in-law. 'I knew it,' she said. 'I knew you'd be in trouble before the day was over. Now I have two invalids to look after. You don't really give a thought to anybody but yourself. You're no good, Bob Archer! What have you done?'

Kathy Manderson dropped the reins which she had been holding for so long in her left hand, and Archer's horse stirred a little as the leathers hit the ground at either side of its drooping head. 'He's done nothing that he wasn't forced into, Anne,' the blonde said. 'If only all men cared as much about others as he does. Treat him right, please. Do you know what you've got there? One of the last heroes of the Old South. When they're gone, there will be only history left.'

Archer couldn't believe what he had heard. He thought the blonde had been juicing him and tried a rueful grin. But then he saw her face as she turned away. Her features were alight with pride. Then he watched her back as she rode off, and he felt a little proud too. The girl had told him all he wished to know.

SIX

It seemed to Bob Archer that pain was less difficult to bear when a man sat in the dark, and that was what he was doing now. It was just after ten o'clock, according to the striking clock which stood on the mantelpiece of the parlour next door, and the night outside his bedroom window was as black as crepe and yet spangled with stars, though a half moon was rising at present behind broken cloud to the southeast and occasionally sent a misty glow across the lower sky. This light filled the windowpanes with cold silver, when it came, and the room about Archer's rocking chair—which had been brought in from the veranda hours ago to meet his need for rest—revealed itself in strange forms, with the bed on his left seeming to acquire the shape of a feeding buffalo, the wardrobe to become a shadowy castle, and the washstand a tent with white guardians standing at either end. It was all quite relaxing, yet seemed a little weird too, and Archer wondered if he could be coming down with a touch of fever.

There was a bowl of cold water standing between his feet. Three folded cloths lay soaking in it, while a large sponge rested on top of his head. From time to time he would press the sponge—which was full of water—and rivulets of chilling liquid would thread across his scalp and then run down his neck and cool his chest and back. Alternately, he would cover his face with one of the cloths and let the influence of the sodden material soothe and reduce the swellings present on his features, the treatment as a whole doing some good—though not much. He had received one hell of a pasting that afternoon, and only time could heal the damage that he had been done. He just hoped, and grimly enough, that Tug Filby was feeling as bad as he. There was some consolation in knowing that he had given an ex-champion snuff. But what the devil had it all been about really? He had achieved exactly nothing and, as if to add insult to injury, he had been dismissed as dirt by Orville Manderson and then led home like a blind man by the rancher's daughter. Failure was failure, and that was also what he felt himself to be. What future good could possibly evolve from any of it?

He shut his eyes. The house was so quiet he could hear tiny rodents running in its foundations. A line of lamplight that shone dimly under his bedroom door told him that his sister-in-law was still up and around. He imagined Anne would burn the midnight oil. She had her husband to consider, and no wife was more caring. The doctor had fixed up Ray's wound nicely, and he was now sleeping under the influence of laudanum, but he had spells of restlessness—audible even in here—and these must be disturbing for Anne and give her little inclination to sleep anyway. There was the worry, too, of the general situation along the strip; for he, Bob Archer, had given the woman an unvarnished account of his activities during the afternoon—and his summing up of what they must mean—so, with all her horror of violence and refusal to accept facts that she didn't want to see as such, she must realize that Orville Manderson was in the ascendancy and that insecurity would be the farmers' lot until the rancher made his big move against their properties. After that—? Well, it didn't really bear thinking about. Not tonight anyhow.

Now a sound impinged on Archer's eardrums. It was in fact the one that he had least expected to hear at this hour, but it was real enough nevertheless. A rider was galloping in from the east and seemed to be making for the Archer farm. The hoofbeats were those of a horse travelling at full stretch, and there was a surging quality about them that suggested a rider on an important errand or even with the fear of being chased. Archer supposed, on reflection, that it could be a combination of both and listened more closely still—his nerves tightening by the moment—then, when the destination of the mount could no longer be in the slightest doubt, he removed the sponge from his crown and dropped it into the bowl between his legs. After that he struggled out of his chair and shuffled across the bedroom, every muscle stiff and aching still, and he opened his door and lurched out into the parlour adjoining, where he saw that his sister-in-law had already left the sofa on which her sewing lay and gone to the front door. This she pulled open, allowing a beam of lamplight to shine out across the floor of the veranda and into the farmyard. At almost the same moment a pale horse arrived in the light, its rider reining back hard and, despite the obscurity around the beam, Archer recognised Kathleen Manderson and her palomino instantly.

Fearing for the girl, though not yet entirely sure why, he held his position at the back of the parlour and let his sister-in-law and the daughter of the Broken M greet each other in the briefest of fashions and watched as Kathy came running into the house and halted at the centre of the parlour, where she stood breathing heavily and rummaging in the inside pocket of the mackinaw which she was wearing to keep out the chill of the night air. 'Bob,' she gasped, acknowledging him with an abstracted glance; and then she fished out a roll of paper that was tied with a purple ribbon. 'I've got it. I stole it from among Mary Lewis's things.'

'The water agreement?' he asked tensely, knowing full well that it could be nothing else.

Holding the roll of paper out to him, Kathy Manderson gave her head an emphatic jerk. 'I couldn't allow my family and that Lewis girl to get away with their wickedness. When that agreement is back with its rightful owners, dad will have to think twice before he cuts the Blood country farmers off from the water in Cold Wells.'

'Well done, Kathy,' Archer said stonily.

'Nobly done, I'd say!' his sister-in-law corrected, eyeing him severely, undoubtedly to let him know that she had picked up the note of unwarranted reservation in his tones. 'And done for us!'

'Sure,' Archer acknowledged. 'She's a brick! But think what she's done to herself. Her pa will skin her alive for this! She'll never be welcome in her own home again.'

'After our adventures this afternoon,' Kathy said, 'I was no longer welcome at my father's table anyhow. Oh, don't look like that! Bringing that agreement back to the farmers was more important than anything that may happen to me because of it.'

'But what is going to happen to you now?' Anne Archer stressed, her perspective on what the blonde had done having clearly shifted into line with her brother-in-law's now that she had had time to consider his fears for Kathy. 'There's no question that by helping us you've alienated yourself from home and family.'

The blonde waved the rolled agreement —which she was still holding out to Archer—in the air beneath his nose. 'Surely you don't want me to leave here and take this back home with me?' she said sharply, sounding mildly outraged and a little hurt.

'Don't be crazy!' Archer implored, the words distorting thickly as they tumbled over his swollen lower lip. 'No such thing!'

'We were only thinking about you, Kathleen!' Anne Archer begged in her turn. 'This is an act of self-sacrifice for which you alone will have to pay the price. We're not ingrates. We thank you for what you've done from the bottom of our hearts! But where will you go now? You could stay with us—and we'd be happy to have you—but I fear that would only prove another act of madness. We're too close to the Broken M.'

'I understand all that,' Kathy said dismissively. 'I haven't been as heedless of my own welfare as you appear to think, Anne. Far from it!' She smiled as Archer now took the water agreement from her hand. 'I shall ride on into Starrville when I leave here. My aunt Betty lives in the town. She's told me before that I can have a home with her whenever I need one. Woe betide dad if he starts throwing his weight about near her. She's no fear of him whatsoever and, like all big sisters, knows the little boy's weak spots.'

'That sounds all right,' Archer commented. 'Do you think anybody up at the Broken M knows what you've done yet? I mean in terms of the theft. You rode in here like the hounds of hell were on your heels!'

'I know I did,' the girl admitted. 'I expect guilt was driving me. I went through Mary's box while she and my brother Jem were out riding. With me gone, the family will probably have looked into the matter and confirmed the fact by now. I think my father was allowing Mary to hang on to the agreement so that she could keep a feeling of security.'

'Or a hold over him?' Archer suggested, well aware of the innate spuriousness involved and knowing that he had implied a true correction. 'The crooked surely understand each other well enough—and that girl couldn't fully trust anybody up there.'

'Including me,' Kathleen observed ironically. 'Well, there it is, for good or ill. If they do know by now back at the ranch, and have anticipated my movements since leaving, it will still take them a while to get down here.'

'Trouble is,' Archer reflected, tapping an end of the ribbon-bound water agreement on the palm of his left hand, 'we don't know how much of a while. I guess I ought to return this paper to Jack Luker right away, but I'm not going to, Kathy. It'd be too easy for your pa to work out where it was and take it back by force. Remember, the gloves are off.'

'What are you going to do with it then?' Anne Archer asked, both her expression and tone of voice daring him to make any kind of stupid reply.

'Put it where it'll be safe,' he answered. 'It's a legal document and entitled to protection from the law. I'll lodge it with the sheriff of Starrville. I reckon he has an office safe, or a strong-box at least.'

'Don't forget Lawyer Hughes,' Kathy Manderson said. 'He has a safe.'

'And premises that seem to fly afire to the disadvantage of his clients,' Archer responded cynically. 'Lawyers, Miss Manderson, ain't a breed I trust. They're a treacherous lot around money. By God, they've caused some trouble in the South since the war, haven't they just!'

'Very well,' the blonde said. 'I leave it to your judgement. I must go.'

'I'm coming with you,' Archer informed her. 'I can't leave you to the mercies of the night. It wouldn't be right.'

'Don't be absurd!' Kathy Manderson protested scornfully. 'I have a saddlegun, I know this country like the palm of my hand, and I can take care of myself perfectly well. Looking at you right now, Bob Archer, I'd say you have a greater need to take care of yourself than I.' She flashed a smile between Archer and his sister-in-law. 'Goodnight you two!'

'Kathy!' Archer exclaimed, putting out a hand to restrain her, but she dodged clear of his fingers and carried on to the front door—pulling it open with the latch and passing outside—then, leaving the woodwork ajar, she hastened down the veranda steps at an audible run and regained a horse which snorted at her presence. After that the animal's hooves clopped as she turned it about and mounted up. Then she galloped off, and within a few moments only the fading noise of her rapid departure echoed back into the living room of the farmhouse.

'This doesn't seem—' Anne Archer began.

'You don't suppose I aim to leave it like that?' her brother-in-law interrupted; and, taking a grip on himself—for he certainly didn't feel up to much—he faced away from Anne and re-entered the darkness of his bedroom. Here he lifted his boots out of the space between the wardrobe and the washstand and stamped them on. Next he took his gunbelt off the back of the cane chair which stood in the rear right-hand corner of the room and swung it around his waist. Then, latching up, he stepped out into the parlour once more and made for the still unfastened front door, only checking again when the watching Anne asked tensely: 'Bob—do you think we'll have visitors?'

'Here? Shouldn't be surprised.' He thought about it for a moment, frowning hard, then added: 'I don't believe you've anything to worry about. If men from the Broken M do come down, they'll only be concerned with locating Kathleen.'

'I hope you're right.'

'I'm sure of it,' he said, though with a confidence that began to ebb the moment he had expressed it—for this business did also include what had become of the water contract since Manderson's daughter had stolen it off Mary Lewis tonight, and that could cause visitors from the Broken M, if under pressure—and they almost certainly would be—to behave in a more intrusive manner than would normally be asked of them. They might insist on searching the farm property from end to end—regardless of the disastrous incident which that could provoke—but he had to remind himself that this affair had only just given way to activities outside the law and Orville Manderson would be unlikely to chance any behaviour that was too blatant as yet. The master of the Broken M was subject to the law, like everybody else, and would be expected to show the evidence of a cast iron case for invading other properties in search of a paper that truly belonged elsewhere. No, he wouldn't risk it; not tonight. So Archer concluded with the words: 'Take it easy, Anne. I'll see you when I see you.' And then he left the house—not with the speed and lightness of foot that Kathy Manderson had demonstrated a few minutes ago, but fast enough for all that.

Again he went to the farm stables—as he had done around the middle of the day—and now he lighted a swinging lantern and got his horse out of its stall, saddling up with all the speed he could generate. That done, he extinguished the light again and led his mount outside, where he stepped into leather and spurred away from the farm buildings towards the dirt path at the northern edge of the property. Joining the track, he headed westwards, hoping to catch up with Kathleen Manderson in due course; but he realized that there was very little chance he would manage this, for her start on him was one of several minutes and her palomino a horse of the first grade that could outrun his more commonplace mount on every day of the year. In circumstances like these, however, a man could only do what his mind prompted and stick with his best intentions. His concern for the girl was genuine, but his chief aim must nevertheless be to carry the water agreement—now stuffed a trifle casually into the back-pocket of his trousers—into town and make sure that it ended the night in a safe place. So he kept his reins lashing and his rowels digging, and a couple of miles soon passed underfoot, with the lamps of the widely spaced farms along the strip shining out at him like the mutest of guides and the moon-whitened night stretching into distances on all hands that were mainly a mingling of fitful shadows edged by fields of absolute darkness. He could indeed have been enclosed just then by the black walls of Pluto's hell.

There was a leaden hush beyond the rhythmic beating of his mount's hooves. This part of the Texas night was like a vacuum yawning to be filled. Then out of the emptiness of it, and sounding not quite human in that moment, came voices raised and quarrelsome—with female tones climbing above the rest, shrill, protesting, and frightened too—and Archer knew from this distant uproar that Kathleen Manderson was in trouble and almost certainly stopped. Checking his horse with a heave of his arms, Archer brought the animal's pace down to little more than a walk in a matter of yards, and he sent his gaze boring ahead of him—judging that, not only had Kathleen's theft been promptly detected back at her home but her intentions had been so accurately anticipated by her father that he had been able to send out a body of men from the

Broken M, over the steep path which cut through the ridge just to the west of Jack Luker's place, and intercept his daughter on the road to Starrville after she had made her call at Ray Archer's farm.

The rancher could have entertained the hope that the girl would still have the water agreement about her when the interception was made, since he might have believed her too intelligent to leave a document of such importance in the dubious care of dim-witted farm folk, even if it did belong to them. Anyway, whatever the possible truth of that, the girl had been caught—unless he was mistaken to an extent that he didn't believe possible—and a search of her horse and person must soon make it plain that she had left the agreement somewhere behind her as she had journeyed up the strip; which would mean that, assuming a second group of riders had been despatched from the Manderson ranch with orders to enter the Blood country over the eastern route,

Kathy's present captors would take her back to these men over the ground that she had recently covered and inform them that the vital document was no longer with her, and that they must search the Archer farm—and the Luker too, if that should prove necessary—with the utmost care for it. That his own name would come into the matter at last, Archer didn't doubt, but he expected to have done something to right the immediate situation before that eventuality could evolve.

With his senses at full stretch, Archer kept his horse moving slowly to the front, and it was only a minute or so later that he made out a cluster of shadowy horsemen directly before him. Now he stopped his mount completely and settled low in his seat, drawing his revolver, for he was conscious that the moon was at his back and that he must already be providing the silhouette of his presence for any one of the men ahead who had remained vigilant enough during the accosting of the girl to watch the ground to the east of the party for anybody else who might come riding up from the direction of the farms.

The only thing that mattered now was to free Kathleen Manderson. There were two ways in which the rescue could be attempted, but neither was all that satisfactory. He could charge down upon the riders yonder, firing his Colt above their heads, in the hope of breaking them up—and thus giving Kathy an opportunity to swing away and flee—or he could try to blend in with the gloom beside the track and jump the party when it was about to draw level with him. He could then call on the blonde to make herself scarce, while he did his best to extricate himself from the problem that he would have created for himself with the ranchmen. Since at this hour, and in this changeful light, it would be impossible for one man to hold the better part of a dozen prisoner for longer than it took for the shock of his initial challenge to wear off. After that any man in the ruck would be able to draw on him and let rip without his seeing a thing of it before it was too late.

Archer steadied himself in his saddle. He reckoned he'd take the charge option. But then he saw that the party up track was now on the move and heading towards him. It was amazing that he had not been spotted before this, but it was certain that whatever he did or did not do in the seconds ahead he would be glimpsed by the oncoming riders; so, feeling now that he would give both Kathy and himself the best chance of escaping the dangerous situation to come by keeping everything at a reasonable distance, he studied the advancing horsemen intently—calculating their position in his plan yard by yard—and he was about to shout a challenge, when a yell went up in the ranch party's front rank and a gun went off—the bang of the shot being followed by several others as accelerating shapes began to surge at him. 'Kathy!' he bawled at the top of his voice.

'Break clear—and get the hell out!'

'Hey, Tug!' somebody was already shouting. 'That blamed gal has high-tailed it! She gave Wesley Johns a cut o' the skull and just—just went!'

'Let her go, g'dammit!' Tug Filby's voice responded. 'That son-of-a-bitch yonder is Bob Archer! He's the one who'll be carrying that durned paper! I want him dead as a doornail—so does the boss! Gun him down!'

Pistolfire snapped and crackled, the detonations oddly dull and thudding against the ground. Archer could detect the underlying hoofbeats amidst the shooting too, for the range was down to well under a hundred yards. He fired back, triggering three times as swiftly as he knew how, and two men toppled from their horses in the van of the charging ranch party, one uttering a scream and the other falling without a sound. Archer deemed his shooting pretty good, all things considered—and would have been happy to share a further exchange—but he knew that he had already delayed plenty long enough at this spot. Thrusting his gun away, he climbed his horse round to the left and set it down on grass, the beast stretching southwards the instant that it felt springy turf underfoot; and away they went, lead chasing them every yard of the way and the scarlet fire streaking from the muzzles of the pursuing guns plucking constantly at the tail of the fleeing man's right eye.

Archer felt no fear just then. He simply let his galloping mount have its head. Into the darkest of the night they dived, the going as flat and easy as a man could wish, and soon mists broke and tugged around them, while the vapours of the east parted in a brief swirling and fused again over the moon, thus creating the same bull's-eye lantern effect on the landscape that the fugitive had remarked a scant hour ago when sitting in his bedroom at his brother's home and enduring his aches and pains in reasonable comfort.

Again he asked himself how the heck he had come to this. For the bodily torture that he was going through with every thump of his mount's shoes against the earth could only be a foretaste of the sufferings of the damned—the prelude to a Saturday morning drop into hell itself!

The firing petered out at Archer's back, and once again the silence of the night fell in upon him from either hand. Craning, he gazed behind him for a long moment, knowing that Tug Filby and company couldn't be far away, but corridors of obscurity mazed back there and mist and moonlight rolled thinly across the more northerly of the land and smudged detail. There was no sign of the pursuit, and Archer had the feeling that—more by luck than judgement—he had already lost the ranch party and probably would not encounter it again tonight. But he kept drubbing southwards nevertheless, allowing his horse to moderate its own pace as it tired, and it wasn't until he realized that he had reached the end of the flat and was now climbing the side of a hill that he asked himself in a new and objective turn of mind if this forward drive of his was any more than the subconscious desire to keep pushing ahead until he had left this district behind him. To do that would suit him fine. He had a bit of money in his pocket and didn't need much of anything to keep him alive. But he still had that water contract on him too. And, if he were to carry on down into the heart of Texas, his action would be as fatal to the farmers of the Blood country as if he were to turn about this minute and ride to the Broken M itself with the intention of putting the document into Orville Manderson's hand. No, for Starrville he had been headed and to Starrville he still must go.

Soon he topped out. Halting his lathered horse on the summit of the hill, he sat in the wind and looked around him at the dim vastness of the plains which had made a few men rich and provided many with their graves. He heard a coyote's plaint, high and echoing, saw a nightbird cross the yellow valleys of the moon, and picked up the faint rustling of mice in the grass. And he was wondering whether to backtrack and angle off to the left, in the hope of cutting a trail that would take him to Starrville, when he made out the lights of human habitations just to the left of where he judged westpoint to be and not too far distant.

Yes, that would be Starrville he was peering at. If he rode down the side of the hill to his right, took a twenty degree turn in the same direction at the bottom, then rode in the straightest line that he could follow, he should reach the town in less than an hour. That was providing, of course, there were no further interruptions to his journey. The Broken M riders and their foreman must still be around and probably within hailing distance of him. They would not have given up as yet. Their boss had not struck Archer as a man who would readily accept just any old excuse for failure; and Filby, knowing that, could well make a guess at where his party's quarry meant to go and throw out scouts accordingly.

The night still had danger in it.

SEVEN

Archer sent his horse down the west face of the hill. Then, no longer assisted by the guiding lights of the town—which were now well below his level of vision and entirely invisible to him—he turned on to his planned course and spurred ahead confidently enough. He kept his speed down, however, and remained watchful, and he moved wide of the slightest sound or movement which reached him out of the encircling gloom. This tendency to caution may well have saved him from running into trouble two or three miles on; for, though he actually saw nothing, he thought he heard horses moving around in a stand of timber that appeared to the right of his path and the baffled growling of a voice in authority. Once more he brought his mount to the stand and sat stockstill himself, eyes and ears straining as on earlier occasions and, only when he was sure that it was again safe to do so did he stir back into life and resume his journey—feeling a considerable relief that nothing worse had manifested which stayed with him until he reached Starrville about half an hour later and let his horse amble into the head of the main street and move down the band of shadow beyond it like a ghost which the lamplight from either hand could not touch.

He entered a small square at the middle of the town. This space seemed to have most of the larger and more important buildings of the place set about it. Archer located the law office on the eastern side of the square. He expected to find an incumbent present but, though oil lamps were burning on brackets at either side of the street door, no sheriff was on duty, and he was left to suppose that Starrville saved itself a little money by only staffing its law office during the day. This was a nuisance, to say the least of it, for Archer knew the danger that the document could be recovered by force and returned to the wrong hands at any time while it was on his person; but there was nothing that he could do about the situation in which he found himself tonight and he could only pray that he would not be located by his enemies before the sheriff came on duty tomorrow morning.

Afoot now and leading his horse in the general hush and darkness at the centre of Starrville, Archer thought about that one for a short while—considering various safe ways in which to spend the night, from requesting a corner at the livery barn, to hiring a hotel room until sunup, or even sitting it out in the blackness at the foot of a fire escape—and he was just getting ready to take up his first option and seek out the town stables, when the sound of footfalls at his back caused him to whirl about and jerk his pistol, but a female voice promptly chided him in tones of the softest mockery, saying: 'Don't kill me, Bob. You might regret it.' Then the speaker tut-tutted. 'You are on edge!'

'Kathy,' he murmured, tempted to reprove her in turn but putting up his gun instead. 'I am on edge, and I would regret it. I've got plenty to be on edge about right now. It's that sort of night, I guess.'

'I was banking you'd show up in the square before the night was over,' Kathy Manderson said. 'I knew you'd soon shake off those addlepates my dad employs. I've been watching for you.'

'Too bad the law locks up at night,' Archer commented. 'It's come to a pretty pass when the sheriff spends the hours in bed when you're likely to need him most. Ain't that just like people for you!'

'Oh, there'd be somebody in the jail-house if a hanging was due, Bob.'

'Why don't that surprise me?' Archer wondered dryly. 'Well, you've found me, girl. What are you going to do with me?'

'Turn you out to grass, I think!' came the jaundiced response. 'Do talk sense, Bob! What do you think I'm going to do with you? I'm going to take you back to Aunt Betty's with me, of course.'

'Should've known,' he admitted contritely. 'Can be a bit of a fool at times, can't I?'

'I wouldn't say that,' the girl said soberly. 'It was as well for me you showed up at the end of the strip when you did. Tug Filby and the boys were about to take me back to your brother's farm when you interrupted things. Without that, the night could have ended up an unholy mess—with God knows what happening!'

'Still could,' Archer reflected. 'Let's get off the street then. I have the feeling Filby and your pa's men could still come through presently. It's the obvious move, sure enough, and I'll stake my life they're still around!'

'Be careful what you do with your life,'

Kathy advised. 'And behave yourself too. I've been talking to Aunt Betty, and she's already on the warpath.'

'That's all we need!' Archer sighed.

The girl faced round. Following the edge of the boardwalk on her left, she headed for the main thoroughfare—Archer leading his mount in her wake—and was about to enter the street itself, when the noise of several horses trotting into the town's southern end became audible and brought Kathy to an abrupt stop. 'That could be them, Bob!' she whispered breathlessly. 'Quick—back into the shadows! Not a sound!'

Archer halted instantly. Easing at his mount's head, he backed the creature up. Now he made out a gap between two buildings on his left. The one to the rear was much the larger structure, and that in front of it hardly bigger than a good-sized shed. But the space between the two offered room enough to make a good hiding place. Archer, still squared up to his mount's jaws, eased the creature round and drew it safely over the boardwalk, murmuring for Kathy to pursue. This she did; then, after stroking and patting his horse into immobility, Archer eased his way back to the corner of their hiding place at the edge of the square and peeped out. He was quite startled, and clapped a hand to the butt of his gun when, as the riders on the main street drew level with the open space on their left, one of their number said: 'I tell you, Tug, I saw somebody along here. Just here—where we are now. It was only the flicker of a shape, man—but there was somebody there.'

'I'm not saying you're wrong, Forbes,' Filby answered. 'But where are they now? D'you see them?'

'How about hid up?'

'Just maybe,' the foreman allowed, his tone of voice emphasizing that his patience with it all was wearing thin. 'All right. We'll give the square the once over.'

'Afoot?'

153

'Please yourself,' Filby said. 'I'm not climbing down.'

There was little doubt that the foreman's followers were all tired out and in much the same mood as he, for nobody dismounted, and the riders turned as a body into the square and made a kind of circuit of it, peering as they went round but missing the corners of the place and the several nooks and alleys where concealment was possible. It was in fact a perfunctory effort, but Archer could only watch the parts of it visible to him in a state of anxiety and tension, and he finally released the pent up air in his lungs and relaxed again when, from the opposite side of the square, he heard Filby sing out: 'I'll say it plain, men. We have no idea where the fellow is. We can't even be sure that he came here. He was heading south when we saw him last. We can't spend the whole night looking into holes and corners where the son-of-a-bitch might be but ain't!'

'So what d'you aim to do about it, Tug?'

the man Forbes enquired.

'That's a good question,' Filby snarled.

'Well, you're the foreman,' came the self-righteous response.

'I am,' Filby agreed, demonstrating true toughness of character through the amount of anger that he was so obviously suppressing as he spoke. 'I have no need to be reminded of it. If we start for home right now, it'll be after two in the morning before we get back to the bunkhouse—and nigh three before we get settled in bed. We have to be up at five. That's a lot short of a night's sleep. You fellows ain't what I'd call champion workers on the best of days, and I have tomorrow's work to consider before all else.'

'Do you mean to say, Tug, all this here riding ain't goin' to count against that?' Forbes questioned, sounding rather peeved.

'Not by one jot!' Filby assured him. 'Orv Manderson has no time for weaklings, and neither have I. I promise you I'll fire any man I find sleeping on the job tomorrow.'

Just then Archer heard a bedroom window fly open at the top of a house not far away, and an angry male voice shouted down into the square: 'Go home, blast your eyes, Filby! Stop pratin' like the king of all the Germans! If you can't sleep yourself, have the goodness to let us sleep!'

'Hold your row, whoever y'are' Filby flung back—'or I'll punch your head tomorrow! If losing a mite of sleep is your only worry, you're blessed!'

'Any more o' that,' came the threat from on high, 'and I'll empty this here shotgun among you!'

'That's Cogman of the general store,' Forbes cautioned. 'He might just do that. We can't take on the whole doggone town!'

'Who said anything about tryin'?' Filby demanded. 'Let's go. The boss'll just have to stamp and swear. Next stop the Broken M!'

The ranchmen headed out of the square, jockeying a little in their haste; then they turned left into the main street—opening up now and gathering pace—and they left town at an illegal gallop, creating sufficient noise to wake up Starrville from end to end. But the clatter of their going soon faded into the north, and the town quickly became silent again.

'They were closer than they knew,' Archer reflected. 'Wouldn't they be sick if they could tell!'

'I can't believe that man saw me,' Kathy Manderson said indignantly. 'He must have the eyes of a cat!'

'It don't matter now,' Archer reminded her, starting to ease his mount backwards into the square again. 'All's well that ends well, eh?'

'What's ended?' the girl asked grimly, sliding out of the space that had concealed them ahead of the horse. 'We're going to Adobe Street.'

'That where Aunt Betty lives?'

'At number six, yes.'

Archer nodded and went on with what he was doing. Then, with his mount standing well out into the open, he caught hold of it at the bit and began walking it after the girl. They turned right on the main street, then rounded the first corner on the left, moving now between rows of dwellings which looked of more consequence than most in the town, and it wasn't long before Kathy Manderson halted at a picket fence—to which her palomino was already hitched—and said: 'Tie your horse up beside mine.' After that she indicated the tall house behind the fence, with its bay windows and steep roof of slates. 'Aunt Betty lives there. Wipe your feet when we go indoors.'

'Always do,' Archer assured her seriously, spinning a hitch on the rail and stifling a yawn. 'Filby ain't the only guy who could do with a sleep, Miss Manderson. Would you believe I came to Ray's farm on vacation?'

area was hardly up to his inches, and the big woman smiled and left him, her tread soon echoing from the nearby stairs as she sought her bed. It was warm in the kitchen—perhaps too warm—but, deciding things could be a heck of a lot worse, Archer drew his revolver and placed it on his lap. Then he folded his arms and shut his eyes, falling soon into an uneasy sleep in which he was conscious of every sound, from near and far, but the night passed by without incident and when he fully awakened again, there was daylight at the window and Betty Manderson and her niece were back in the kitchen with him. 'What's the time?' he yawned, sitting up stiffly and rasping at his stubbly jaw.

Aunt Betty pointed towards the mantel-piece, where a carriage clock stood.

Archer followed her finger, and saw that the clock showed a quarter to six. 'What time does your sheriff open his office, ladies?'

'Buck Stevens isn't what you'd call a

rigid man,' the big woman said. 'He's no stickler for time. I rate him a lazy devil. Oh, he knows how many beans make five all right, and he's good at his job, but he works no harder than he has to.'

'Don't sound like you're all that keen on him,' Archer said carefully, turning his feet to the floor and thrusting his Colt back into its holster.

'Speak your mind, boy,' Aunt Betty encouraged crisply—'speak your mind.'

'I don't doubt you have your reasons for what you say,' Archer said more purposefully, 'but you worry me a bit. I've met plenty of men who function like your sheriff, but nobody bothers much. What's more, if you'll pardon me, you haven't quite answered my question.'

'It could be anywhere between six and seven o'clock,' Betty Manderson replied. 'I believe I said last night, Kathy told me what your business here is.'

'You think I'd be wiser to take it elsewhere,' he stated.

'She's not sure,' Kathy Manderson put in, drawing a tortoiseshell comb through her blonde tresses. 'Buck Stevens is a difficult man to ever be sure about. He's kind of arbitrary—if you know what that word means?'

'I know what it means,' Archer said, standing up and grimacing at the battered face which the mirror hanging above the mantelpiece showed him. 'No oil painting is right,' he confessed between thoughts. 'So your sheriff likes the first word and the last, eh?'

'He's inclined to play God,' the big woman said, upgrading Archer's interpretation by more than somewhat. 'The law has a lot of power in an out-of-the-way place like this. Be careful of him, that's all. He's my brother's friend. He even owes his appointment to Orville.'

'Who the deuce can you trust?' Archer asked, giving way to a momentary blurt of anger. 'You've knocked me all of a heap! The nearest real law is in Dallas,

I reckon. That's a hundred and fifty miles from here.'

'You're not going there,' Kathy said firmly.

'I'm not going there,' he agreed. 'I'll take my chances in Starrville. The farmers out on the strip have an incontrovertible case. There's another big word for you.'

'What if my father could bring doubt into it?' Kathy queried.

'He can't,' Archer said, his utterance so downright that even he was startled by it for a moment.

'Don't tempt Providence, Mr Archer,' Aunt Betty cautioned with a gravity that, for all her normal confidence, was perhaps the voice of the true woman.

Archer put a hand into the back-pocket of his trousers. He brought out the water agreement which he was still carrying there and untied the short length of purple ribbon which kept the document rolled up. After that he unrolled the sheet of yellow and ageing foolscap on the top of the kitchen table and weighted it open at the bottom and top with the presence of his hands. The penwork on the paper was good, if rather faded, and there was not a great deal of it. Archer read:

Concluded this day. April 21st, 1849, an agreement between Shamus Manderson, of the Broken M ranch, and Peter Blood, of Blood farm, both in Falls County, North Texas.

In consideration of permanent grazing rights on the eastern meadows of the Blood lands—approximately one thousand acres in extent—the water supply known as Cold Wells is transferred to Peter Blood, for his own use and that of his heirs and successors, in the same permanency as the grazing rights noted above.

Signed by:
Shamus Manderson, Peter Blood.

'Plain enough, ladies,' Archer said, moving

aside, while continuing to hold the paper flat, and giving the two women the opportunity to scan what he had just read. 'In fact "cut and dried" is the phrase that comes to mind.'

'I had read it before,' blonde Kathy admitted. 'It is about as simple and straightforward as these things can get.'

'Yes,' Aunt Betty admitted, but she still sounded unsure. 'That baby brother of mine will ride roughshod if he believes he can get away with it. On the other hand, whatever he does usually has some basis in law. He's given to folly but not stupidity. There could still be something written there that he can use.'

'What?' Archer asked bluntly, rolling the paper up again and tying it with the piece of ribbon.

'I don't know.'

Archer returned the document to his back-pocket. He no longer had any good feeling about what was to come, and he experienced an urgent desire to get it all over with as quickly as possible. 'Look, it's rising six o'clock. I'm going to walk along to the law office right now. I'll take a chance on the sheriff being around by the time I get there.'

'I'm coming with you,' Kathy said.

'My dear,' her aunt said quietly, reaching out and touching her in the bend of her left arm, 'I think you would do wisely to keep out of it this morning. You've done your part. It's up to other people now.'

'Your aunt's right, Kathy,' Archer said seriously. 'All you can do now is enrage your pa further. The farmers are well and truly in your debt, and so am I. Sadly, such debts are too seldom acknowledged—and almost never repaid.'

'I don't expect to be repaid,' Kathy said shortly, 'and I don't care if what I've done is never acknowledged. As far as I can, I want to live right and see justice done.'

'If there's a heaven,' Archer sighed, 'you'll likely get there. If there ain't, you'll mebbe live happier than most. But—leave it at that, will you?'

'All right,' the girl said, looking and sounding a little hurt.

'We'll have breakfast waiting for you when you get back,' Betty Manderson informed him briskly, 'and we'll be anxious to learn how the sheriff reacted to what you had to tell him.'

'All I want the man to do is take the water agreement off my hands,' Archer responded, 'and put it somewhere safe. If I get that much done, I'll be satisfied.'

He gave his forelock a tug. Then he left the kitchen and the house, giving his horse—which was still standing at the picket fence—a pat on the rump in passing. A minute later he re-entered the main street and walked on into the square, moving straight across it and towards the law office, which had an open front door and mounts secured to the rail outside it.

The sight—which in fairness did not have to mean what Archer so strongly suspected it meant—filled him instantly with dismay, and he was tempted to turn about and make a swift return to Adobe Street—before everything blew up in his face—but he reminded himself that the man who reversed course in a situation like this could only be a coward, and he had never been that. So he walked on and entered the office, where he immediately saw a handsome, moustachioed man with an exceptionally well-developed torso lounging rather theatrically behind the desk, and at his back, sitting on a small table and picking his nails with a Bowie knife, a heavy-set deputy who wouldn't see fifty again. To the right of this scene, seated on straight-backed chairs placed against the wall where a pot-bellied stove raised its chimney-pipe to the ceiling between the office gun cupboard and the maps of the district, were Orville Manderson, a younger man and a dark, quick-eyed girl, while on either side of this trio, erect—and with the badly cut, bruised, and exhausted-looking foreman standing to the left—were Tug Filby and a flinching, crafty-eyed Jack Luker.

'Would you be Bob Archer?' asked the big man behind the desk, moving to bring the star on the front of his shirt into prominence.

'Reckon you know that well enough,' Archer acknowledged, realizing that, in some shape or form, his worst fears were almost certainly on the brink of fulfilment.

'Well, I'm mighty glad you're not denying it,' the sheriff said, smirking into a hand. 'You're late, Archer. We've been waiting this half an hour for you to show up.'

'Seems to me I'd have done better to have called on you in the early hours,' Archer ground in response.

'Be that as it may,' the sheriff said easily, his manner containing the mockery of a man who knew himself to be in absolute control of the situation and was enjoying the enraged bafflement of the man opposite him. 'I understand you have something on you that belongs to Mr Manderson.'

'This, I suppose?' Archer snarled defiantly, flicking the water agreement out of his back pocket and waving it in the air.

'Give it back to him,' the sheriff ordered.

'I'll see all of you at the devil first!' Archer declared, turning smartly on his heel and preparing to leave by the same door through which he had come in.

EIGHT

On reaching the threshold, Archer made to thrust the water agreement into the back-pocket of his trousers again, but his movements were abruptly frozen by the not unexpected sounds of a revolver being cocked at his back. 'One step more,' the sheriff warned, 'and, sure as my name is Buck Stevens, I'll cut your spine in two!'

Turning once more, Archer faced back into the office. 'What have we got here?' he asked, looking straight into the muzzle of the sheriff's Colt forty-four. 'As pretty a nest of damned crooks as you're ever likely to come across!'

'Give that document back to Mr Manderson,' Sheriff Stevens commanded. 'I won't tell you a third time. Don't make me stir up Starrville with a gunshot at this hour.'

'You're not going to fire that gun, Stevens,' Archer said, tossing his head disdainfully at the lawman. 'I can't say I like the look of your deputy a lot, but he might turn out to be half way honest. You never can tell about murder.' Moving to his right, he crossed the office floor, holding out the water agreement ahead of him, but instead of handing it to Orville Manderson, he extended it to Jack Luker. 'This is yours, I believe?'

'Too right' Luker muttered, snatching the document from Archer's fingers.

But then the young man sitting at Manderson's side reached out and plucked the water contract from Luker's grasp, passing it to the girl on his left. 'Yours, Mary.'

The girl nodded—then extended her right arm and gave the slender roll of paper to Orville Manderson. 'Yours, sir.'

'Mine indeed,' the rancher agreed smugly.

'How d'you make that out?' Archer demanded, well aware that, in the present circumstances, there didn't have to be a reply to his question, honest or otherwise.

'Were you born without sense, Archer?' Jack Luker almost spat. 'Didn't I tell you? Peter Blood made me his heir.'

'I believe you did,' Archer admitted, suddenly perceiving that he had been blinded to the simple truth by his own concept of loyalty to his friends. 'The heir becomes the owner of what's willed to him, eh? Ain't you a dirty skunk!' He considered the pretty, quick-eyed girl who sat with the young man who could only be Jem, Orville Manderson's son. 'Even worse, I reckon. A consorter with scheming whores. What's your missus think to that, Jack? I guess you were down on the hearth, giving Mary Lewis what for, while Mrs Luker was lying nearby at death's door. Figures that water agreement had to be regarded as a consideration once the girl had a hold over you. I reckon she took that document as openly as you like, and you had to let it happen.' His expression became one of disgust for all concerned. 'It looks to me like a high price those farming fellows of yours are about to pay for your pleasure, Mr Luker.' Now he pointed at the young man who still had to be definitely identified as the heir to the Broken M. 'As for you, mister, I understand Mary Lewis is your intended. I wouldn't touch her with a cattle prod!'

'Jem!' the girl pleaded, sounding out-raged; but, instead of springing to his feet and trying to knock Archer to the floor—as she so clearly wished of him—the young Manderson, big and muscular enough for anything, simply looked uncomfortable and turned his eyes to the floor. He sat rigidly, his true indifference to the plight of the clearly 'used' female at his elbow starkly revealed. 'Oh, Jem!'

'Be quiet, Mary!' Orville Manderson snapped at her, carefully putting the paper tied about with ribbon into the inside pocket of his coat. 'You have a job in my house. What more do you want?'

'He told me he loved me, sir!' Mary Lewis gulped, the tears beginning to flow. 'Jem instructed me how to get that document, and I was sure you were behind it. He said he'd disregard whatever I had to do to get it. Reckoned he wasn't a prude. Not much! He's just like every fellow who's had his sweets; he don't want any sours. How could you-all treat a poor girl so?'

'You silly mutt!' Archer chided, not without a trace of sympathy in his disdain, for the servant girl had no doubt been a trusting soul in her way. 'Brought up in an orphanage, weren't you? Didn't you learn there that the likes of us don't even count with folk like them? They've got money, Mary—lots of it!—and that makes them think they're better than human and us less. A working girl can never trust a Jem Manderson and his family. But what's the good o' talking? It's all

179

too late. The deed's done. You'll never be trusted again—by anybody, high or low. Fool's gold, Mary, and it's left you worthless!'

The girl snuffled and sniffed, cringeing away from him, then showed her teeth and spat out: 'You shut up, you horrible man! Everybody says you're the biggest idiot around! I hope they hang you!'

'I'd bet my bottom dollar the Yankees will!' the sheriff promised her. 'Bob Archer has been identified as a man badly wanted by the heads of the military government. He's a known vigilante—the leader of that Sadd River bunch. He's an important arrest.'

'It should keep you in office for years, Buck,' Orville Manderson said dryly.

'Can't do me any harm, Orville,' Stevens acknowledged brazenly. 'Might even get me a place among those riding marshals they're talking about up north.'

'Never can tell your luck, Sheriff.'

'Archer must have been plumb crazy to

come here,' Stevens persisted. 'He was asking for it.'

'Thank Jack Luker for putting the finger on him,' the rancher said.

'Treachery,' Archer said bitterly, 'like everything else, is where you find it. But it seems to me right always wins through in the end. So I'm not worrying too much.'

'Tell that to George Maledon when he puts the rope around your neck!' the sheriff advised scornfully. 'Might's the only right, mister—whatever form it takes—and well we all know it!' He snapped his fingers over his shoulder at his deputy, who was still picking his nails with the point of his Bowie knife and had up to then been giving a fair impression of being as deaf as a post. 'Robert Archer is under arrest, Hubert. Disarm him, give me his gun, and lock him up. We'll send word to Dallas that we have him under lock and key when the telegrapher comes on duty at seven o'clock.' He raised an eyebrow at the rancher, then added: 'I reckon that concludes our business for the minute, eh?'

'Why, yes, I think it does,' Manderson concurred, rising to his feet and holding his ground as the deputy—moving fast for a man of his age and weight—rounded the nearer end of Stevens's desk and jerked the prisoner's revolver, dropping it on the woodwork in front of the sheriff with a considerable thud. After that, plucking his own sixgun out of leather, the deputy threatened Archer's back and gave him a shove between the shoulder-blades. 'The cells are that way,' he gravelled out, and Archer caught a glimpse of the cages in the cell block through a stone doorway set in the rear wall of the office. 'Pick 'em up!'

Then, as he essayed his first pace towards imprisonment, Archer heard Manderson say: 'I fear this is going to upset that daughter of mine badly. Why didn't you keep riding? America is a very big country, Archer, and it has many hiding places.'

'An honest man doesn't need to hide,'

Archer threw back over his shoulder, though he felt the response to be a weak one.

'That's something else for him to tell the executioner!' Buck Stevens haw-hawed. 'I'll being seeing you, Orville. Likely before the day's out—up at the Broken M. I'll need a statement from you.'

'Right,' Manderson returned, and Archer heard the rancher leading his party back outside as he began moving ahead of the deputy sheriff towards the prison house.

The deputy unlocked the first cell they came to on the right of the cell block's central passage and shoved Archer into it. 'Best accommodation we got,' he was informed. 'Don't reckon you'll be staying with us all that long, though. I expect the prison waggon will get here the day after tomorrow. If you're lucky, you'll get your trial and swing at Fort Worth.'

'All right, Hubert!' the sheriff called through in a bored voice. 'Just lock him in. You don't have to wise him up. Let him sweat.'

'Whatever you say, Sheriff,' the deputy answered dutifully, slamming the cage door on the prisoner and turning the key. 'Behave yourself, Archer, and you'll find us fair men. Give us a hard time, and we'll give you the same. Remember, we're the ones best fixed to get tough. Savvy?'

'Betcha,' Archer assured him resignedly, testing out the mattress on his chain-slung bunk with a lowered hand. 'I ain't hard to get on with.'

'We'll see,' the deputy said.

'Get back out here, Stone!' the sheriff ordered now. 'Next thing, you'll be telling him his rights.'

'Don't I have any, Stevens?' Archer inquired, moving up to the door of his cell and angling his gaze to meet that of the senior lawman, who was looking into the prison house from around the side of the doorway which connected it with the office.

'Not in here you don't,' the sheriff informed him arrogantly. 'And you call me Sheriff or Mr Stevens.'

'So long as I don't have to call you sir,' Archer said indifferently. 'Sheriff or Mr Stevens will suit me down to the ground.'

'You're a real Texan,' Stevens declared— 'all mouth and britches!'

'You're not?'

'Not what?' the lawman dared.

'A real Texan.'

'God help us, no, smart arse!' the sheriff ground in reply. 'I was born over in Arkansas.'

'They sure must be proud o' that!' Archer reflected good-naturedly, winking at the deputy, who was backed up against the bars of the cage on the opposite side of the central passage and clearly fighting inward laughter.

'Don't you dare, Hubert Stone!' the sheriff cautioned. 'The last deputy who took a rise out of me was out of a job that Saturday!'

'You're the boss, Buck,' Stone assured him, sounding pained as he ambled submissively out of the jailhouse. 'But it's all very well to tell him this an' that, suh. We do have to obey the rules.'

'What the hell do you mean?'

'Follow the book,' the deputy explained innocently. 'He's got the right to be fed. I don't figure he's had breakfast.'

'What the—the deuce does that matter?' the sheriff spluttered. 'He's already too chirpy for a jailbird. Have you eaten, Archer?'

'No, I haven't, and my guts are rumbling,' Archer replied. 'Your deputy is right. The town pays for me to be fed.'

'I'd starve the sass out of you,' Stevens said viciously. 'Fact is, though, we have to keep your weight up if the rope's to do a nice clean job.'

'I like ham and eggs,' Archer said, nodding lugubriously. 'I'm real partial to fried bread and pancakes too. Coffee I can drink by the pot.'

'We can always put poison in it,' the sheriff fired back.

'Wouldn't that spoil it for the rope?'

'Don't push it, Archer!'

'Just trying to keep my spirits up, Mr Stevens.'

'That's enough!' the sheriff announced. 'Save your lip for the Yankees. Settle down. You'll get breakfast at eight o'clock, when the restaurant opens. Now don't bother us, and we won't bother you.'

'It's a deal,' Archer acknowledged, retreating from the door of his cell and stretching himself out full-length on his bunk, for he realized that this was a situation which could be ameliorated but not cured.

Closing his eyes, Archer shut out the ugliness of his prison and summoned the beauty of Kathleen Manderson to his imagination. The girl would indeed be dismayed by his arrest, though it ought not to come as a complete surprise to her. If they had been less tired and fuzzy-witted last night, they might have anticipated the prompt actions by the girl's father which had put him behind bars. Yet even if they had seen it clearly, he would probably have visited the sheriff anyhow, relying on Buck Stevens to accept the facts surrounding the water agreement and do the right thing. No, it had not been possible to be certain of how the sheriff would behave. Aunt Betty had spoken of the man as Orville Manderson's friend—and plainly hadn't trusted him—but even she had not been sure of what he would do.

Everything had, of course, gone about as badly as it could go. He, Archer, was caught, and likely to remain so. In the past he had envisaged a situation like this—particularly on the night that the Sadd River Vigilantes had disbanded—and he had believed himself too smart to ever end up this way, In the event, however, he had not been so clever, and had blundered into what amounted to the simplest of traps. If this business went to a finish, it could see him hanging by his neck from the gallows beam. And many would say, justly too. He had done some wild and dreadful things in his time, and killed a lot of men—most of whom had badly needed killing. All this he could justify to himself in the names of justice and the Old South, but even those who had been friendly to him when it had mattered would probably take the view today that the past was past and he had extended loyalty and duty into sheer revenge. Had he gone too far? It seemed to him, in this moment of despair, that he had. Those who lived badly died the same.

Yet there was still defiance in him. This was not a perfect world, and it had no perfect solutions. He recalled how Anne Archer, his sister-in-law, had been as violent in her pacifism as he had been in his resentment of wickedness. She had been right on her level, for it was true that force only had destructive power if it met actual resistance. Otherwise the energy released only dissipated itself. But Anne Archer's attitude towards him had gone much deeper than that, hadn't it? She had been trying to say that a guy who'd lived as he had lived couldn't one day cry halt and mend his evil ways. There was a momentum which kept plunging onwards through that other world in which the mind and spirit lived. Anne had been seeking to suggest that he was a magnet and would only draw trouble here. Well, it had happened—much too quickly—and the promise of the gun *was* death. But Orville Manderson was a fact on every level too, and the rights and wrongs of the water dispute were plain enough. He had had to be opposed, and would still succeed if others didn't brace him. Manderson's greed and ambition were monsters that could never be satisfied. They could only be killed. And if the man whom they animated had to be slain with them? There was further proof that it was not a perfect world, but merely one of 'be done by as you did.'

Archer's mind shifted a little and his thoughts became lighter. He wondered whether Kathy Manderson would be allowed to visit him during the day—though he had no idea what he would say to her if she did show up. They had met less than twenty-four hours ago, yet he already had the feeling that he had known her for years. Folk talked about love at first sight—and what had happened to him seemed to be an example of it—but he doubted if the girl felt that deeply for him, if at all, since his emotions had been accelerated by the shock of what had happened to him during the last hour or so. Anyway, a relationship between them—even if you took out the fact that Kathy was in every respect his social superior—could have little chance of blossoming, since his future could probably be reckoned in no more than weeks from this date. The Yankees would try him before a military court as quickly as they could, and he'd be sentenced on the same day—and dead and buried within two. So it would be as well if the girl felt nothing for him beyond a friendly fondness. At least, the cemetery at Fort Worth would be too far away to see her putting flowers on his grave. Oh, what the heck! Kathy was too young to grieve, and men should be the least of her problems. There'd be some handsome, honourable, sweet-smelling beau riding up the river for her before long—rot his guts!

Archer was still smiling wryly to himself over that one, when Hubert Stone, the deputy sheriff, entered the jailhouse, calling attention to his presence with a quick whistle. 'I've got your breakfast,' he announced.

Rising from his bunk, the prisoner went to the door of his cell—which had a lateral slot built in above the lock for the purpose of passing in meals and small objects—and took the covered tray which

Stone was now holding half way through the aperture. 'Thank you.'

'You've got your ham and eggs and a mug of coffee,' the deputy informed him. 'We're allowed to feed but not spoil you. I'll find you up some reading later. Unless the sheriff says not.'

'Decent of you anyhow,' Archer said sincerely enough, looking into the uncompromising honesty of the deputy's big, weathered face, with its large bent nose, networks of veins and wrinkles, and dry, cracked lips.

'You ran a good race, boy,' Stone said softly.

'I hope it ain't over yet.'

'That's another kettle of fish altogether,' Stone commented, frowning. 'You broke the Eleventh Commandment.'

'Yeah,' Archer chuckled despite himself —'I got caught.'

'It was this man's army too.'

'Those first parades up in Richmond were surely something,' Archer recalled. 'I never saw so many men on the march.'

'Cold Harbour did it for me. I was a lonely man after that fight.'

'All over a tavern, a well, and a crossroads.'

'There were thousands of dead, and so much blood around you could skate on the grass.'

'The Union caught a licking there.'

'So did we, Archer,' Stone said, turning away with a smile that was grim and sad—'so did we.'

'I was higher up the line, Stone, but I heard what you guys went through.'

'Know you did,' the deputy said, without craning. 'But it makes no never-mind here.'

Of course it made no never-mind here. Archer was not expecting favours. The deputy had to do his job. That was how it should be, and Archer wouldn't have wished it otherwise. Yet Stone still had that sense of brotherhood. He could see the prisoner as an old comrade rather than

194

a felon. That made Archer's lot easier to bear. Whatever the tribulation to come, it would be some consolation to know that there were still good folk around who had felt the glory of the Old South and had the understanding to grasp that the Sadd River boys had been concerned with far more than hell-riding.

Now he withdrew to his bunk and ate his breakfast with the blunted spoon supplied. Then he set his tray aside and, sinking back and putting his hands behind his head, gave himself up to the leaden stillness of the jailhouse. Time dragged by, as was perhaps inevitable, and he went through moments where fear threatened to make his ordeal worse. The sense of being utterly contained worked on his nerves and soon had him pacing the two or three yards of floor that were available to him, but the exercise didn't help much.

He was fed again at noon, and the day outside was warm enough to give him a choky feeling; but this passed off when Hubert Stone brought in a bundle of dog-eared novels and a weekly newspaper. He tried to read, but could not concentrate. He kept wondering why no relative or friend—particularly Kathy Manderson—had been near him. He asked finally about the visiting arrangements, and was told that there were rules governing these. Nobody had as yet applied to see him, but even if they had, the sheriff would have turned them away, for no prisoner was allowed a visitor during the first twenty-four hours after his arrest. This seemed to clear up one thing but kept the other open; and he was left wondering whether perhaps word of his imprisonment had not gone round; but he couldn't believe that. Any form of bad news travelled fast—often because it was seen as good in some quarters. Then, a few minutes after the office clock had clanked off five p.m, the sheriff himself—who had been off duty since the middle of the morning, and was now back to relieve Stone from duty until the early hours—entered the cell block and dropped a bombshell of sorts. He informed the prisoner that he had received official word, via the telegraph office, that the prison waggon—which made regular trips around the territory to pick up captives for transport to the state penitentiaries or superior courts—was in fact ahead of schedule on its rounds and only fifteen miles from Starrville. It should arrive outside Stevens' jail at the breakfast hour tomorrow. That meant that Archer would be borne out of town and away into the country without receiving the chance to say 'farewell' to anybody. Now that wanted a bit of accepting, and it left the prisoner sitting stunned and unhappy on his bunk as the light began to fade. If the past day had seemed long and depressing, Archer perceived that the coming night was going to seem even longer and downright stressful.

Twilight came. Now the sheriff entered

the cell block and lighted the lamps, returning to his office again. Archer tried to shake off his low spirits—conscious that the feeling of neglect which possessed him was not worthy of recognition and even irrational—and he was on the verge of convincing himself that he was to blame for getting himself into trouble and that was that, when he heard voices raised in the office and realized that Kathy Manderson and her Aunt Betty were out there arguing loudly with Sheriff Stevens about what they declared were the 'absurd rules' which governed the arrangements for visiting prisoners. Indeed, so heated did the exchange become that a really serious quarrel might have been sparked off, but the hot words were suddenly drowned out by a terrific explosion nearby and a flash so vivid that it lighted up the gloaming outside with a brightness approaching that of day. The glow soon faded, however—though not by much—and it was at once apparent that a considerable fire was now blazing only a short distance to the left of the law office.

Archer heard running feet. He listened intently and formed the impression that the front of the building was emptying. The sheriff and his visitors were obviously vacating the office itself to find out what had just occurred. Then his attention was diverted by a stranger—a dark, young man who came into the cell block searching through a bunch of keys which he jingled in the process. The newcomer was obviously hunting among the numbered keys for the one that fitted the lock to Archer's cage. Finding it, the young man quickly unlocked the prisoner's door and hissed: 'Out of it! Head for the square!'

Archer needed no second urging. Passing his rescuer in the jailhouse passage, he sprang out into the office and made for the street door.

NINE

Driven by the urge to escape and to blazes with everything else, Archer plunged headlong out of the law office and into the gathering night, almost colliding with somebody who was a good deal smaller than himself. 'Kathy?' he gasped, catching at her and peering closely.

'No!' she insisted, shaking him off. 'Go! Nothing else matters! Aunt Betty rode your horse here! See—it's at the rail!'

Archer had already spotted the animal, which was visible in the light from the lamps which were burning once again upon their brackets at either side of the law office door. Breaking the mount's tie, he swung into his saddle and heaved back on the beast's mouth, climbing his horse away from the hitching rail and dumping its forelegs down in the open square. 'Where is your aunt?' he called back to Kathy.

'Just go!' she blazed at him, her face gaping up at him in what amounted to a half-uttered scream.

He went, driving his heels into his mount's flanks and sending it across the space before him like a missile. Down the square they clattered, with Archer yanking to the left when they reached the main street, and his heart almost tore itself loose in his chest as he fetched back hard on the reins and jinked, narrowly avoiding a succession of collisions with people who had just emerged from the houses on either side of him. These milling folk had obviously been shocked by the recent explosion and were trying to reach the nearby conflagration as swiftly as they could—since it was unlikely that Starrville had a fire engine and manpower and buckets of water were most probably all that stood between the blaze and this wooden town burning down. In this Archer found relief, for people with such an enormous threat hanging over their heads would be unlikely to give a tinker's cuss about the escape of a prisoner from the jailhouse. In fact it could well be morning before anybody gave him another serious thought.

Archer saw a few more folk ahead of him moving rather uncertainly, and he went on exercising a certain amount of care until they were behind him; then, in the clear, he flogged his horse up the remainder of the street and put the limits behind him less than half a minute later. Now he made out open land before him as a black sheet under the glimmering stars and the misty glow of the coming moon.

He picked up his head, determined to travel fast but avoid making any mistake. His problem in that moment was to make up his mind in a hurry what he was going to do next. His money and the other small possessions in his pockets had been taken from him in a jailhouse search, and he was thus without any means of self-support—since he couldn't even live off the country without the gun that had, of course, also been taken from him. It would be crazy even at this juncture to simply live for the moment and gallop off in any direction at all in his denuded state. He must have something in his pocket to live on until he could sort his life out and start anew. Yes, he could steal what he needed—and he would certainly do that if he absolutely had to—but theft so often led to more serious crimes, and he could do without a pursuit of ever-increasing size building up at his rear. No, a criminal who was going to make good his escape must avoid committing new crimes, and a clean ride to freedom in his circumstances was dependent on being able to produce the wherewithal and meet his own needs when necessary. Before he did anything else he must go to his brother's farm, beg a sack of grub and a couple of Eagles, grab any available gun, wish all in sight love and success, then get the hell. Over the Red River might be best. If he never saw these parts again, it would be no great loss—to him or anybody else.

But he wasn't much over a mile out of town when he glimpsed a fair-sized body of riders surging into his path from the right and heard his Christian name called by a familiar voice. Thus, forced to it, he reined back hard and skidded his mount to a halt. 'That you, Raymond?' he demanded in a low shout.

'Yeah, son,' came the response at a similar level—'who'd you expect it was?'

'You're an Archer all right!' Bob declared disgustedly. 'You should be in bed and resting, you blamed idiot! If you pick up an infection in that wound of yours, you'll be headin' a procession before you know it!'

'You always were a cheerful son-of-a-gun, Bob!' his brother informed him. 'And after all the trouble we've gone to springing you from jail!'

'You lovely man!' Archer snorted. 'I'll

allow Kathy Manderson had as much to do with it as anybody!'

'You know she did!' Ray Archer confirmed, inching his horse up close to his brother's and sitting with the kind of one-armed awkwardness which made his silhouette look angular. 'She's worth her weight!'

'She sure is!' Bob agreed fervently, screwing round in his seat and tilting an ear towards the trail as he heard a single horse drubbing towards them from the direction of town, where he could see fire smudging the sky above barely visible rooftops. 'Who the devil is that riding up? I hope to heck it's not that fellow Buck Stevens!'

'No, I reckon it's Fergus Dean,' Ray answered. 'He's one of the young guys from along the strip. Timothy Dean's son. A real able kid, that one, and brave as a lion!'

'Was he the one who got me out of jail, Ray?'

'That's what he parted from us to do.'

'Then he's all you say he is,' Bob Archer said, 'and any other good thing that anybody else wants to say about him.'

'Hell, we figured freeing you was a job best done by one man,' Archer explained. 'It was mostly my plan, though. I hatched it after Kathleen Manderson rode out to my farm this morning with the news that you'd been thrown in jail. I had my boy Harry carry word of it along the strip to everybody there. He told your story, what had gone wrong for you on behalf of the farmers—how it had all come about—and whatever else they wanted to know. After that the farmers came along with their sons and we had a pow-wow in my yard and thrashed out what was to be done. Kathy Manderson was there, too—with additional word from Hubert Stone, the deputy sheriff, spoken by him innocent as you like—that the sheriff himself would be on watch alone in his office during the evening. We could see that would be the time to strike, and all agreed that it was going to be necessary to create a diversion so that somebody could get into the jailhouse this evening and free you. Kathy volunteered her own and her aunt's help to keep the sheriff occupied while young Fergus set up the rest to get Buck Stevens away from his office for a few minutes. Fergus Dean put a couple of sticks of dynamite under the shed where Silas Cogman, who runs the general store, keeps his tanks of coal oil and the like, then lit his fuses.'

The horseman whom Bob Archer had heard riding up a short while before had joined the party of farm riders a minute or so back without any fuss and the barest recognition only. He had sat listening to Ray Archer's talk on the back of his blowing mount, but now he spoke up for himself, a laugh behind his voice as he announced: 'It all worked like a charm! Cogman's lamp oil went up a treat—just like a mortar going off! One hell of a blaze! But it should be awright—'cos the fire's on open ground and there ain't much risk to the buildin's around it. I had a peep at the scene before I rode off. Buck Stevens was runnin' about like a chicken with its head cut off. He was no good at all—not gettin' a blamed thing done—and just weren't able to sort of figure it out. He'll be fit to be tied when he finds he's lost his special prisoner and been made to look a fool!'

There was laughter from every mouth among the shadowy riders bunched up at the side of the trail, and several comments to the effect that Sheriff Buck Stevens hadn't needed much help to prove himself a fool. Not that Bob Archer had quite such a low opinion of the lawman, and there was a trace of anxiety in his tones as he asked: 'Are Kathy Manderson and her aunt going to come out of this okay, boy?'

'Buck Stevens won't be able to prove a thing against 'em,' Fergus Dean answered. 'Stands to reason he'll suspect, don't it?

But there'll be nothin' he can speak of that can be sworn to by a witness. So far as he was concerned, I reckon, the women were with him every moment, and he never saw me.'

'Women always have the edge,' Bob Archer agreed, 'and a thing has to be proved. That Hubert Stone ain't a bad fellow either—and what he said about the work roster was no doubt something he thought didn't matter.'

'Yeah,' Ray Archer drawled, 'I'll buy that, brother! So what d'you aim to do now?'

'Sling my hook,' Bob replied honestly enough. 'Leech off you a mite in the process, I reckon. What you'd expect of a ne'er-do-well like me—I hope.'

'What's mine is yours, Bob,' Ray said simply. 'Sure, you can't do much now but hightail it.'

'Guess it was never going to work out, eh?' Bob regretted. 'Me as a farmer!'

'Couldn't quite see it so,' his elder

brother admitted. 'When you rode in, I had you down as a lazybones lookin' for a rest.'

'Reckon you can say that again!' Bob acknowledged wryly, seeming to confess that he was guilty as charged; but he doubted if any man present knew what it was like to feel tired in the very marrow of the soul—as if sold out with sale day still to come. 'Never done an honest day's work in my life, have I?'

'Not your style at all,' his brother agreed. 'It takes all kinds, so they tell me.'

Bob stirred his mount. 'Do we go back to the farm, Ray?'

'No, I came prepared for this,' Ray answered. 'I've got twenty dollars for you, and a sack of grub. Will it do?'

'It'll serve,' Bob said. 'All I need's enough to get me over the Red and away. Have you got a pistol there. That's maybe my greatest need.'

'You'll have to have mine,' Ray said. 'I've got my saddlegun.'

'I'm sorry about my part in all this,' Bob Archer said, taking the revolver that his brother passed to him and then waiting to receive the two other items for which his brother had begun rummaging about rather uncertainly. 'I still have my doubts that you men know all there is to know. I'll be leaving you in a mess! Orville Manderson has that water agreement in his possession. The law took it off me this morning and it ended up in his pocket.'

'We know about that,' Ray Archer said, ceasing the search around himself in this deeper interest. 'Manderson called at his sister's home in town and did a little crowing over his daughter Kathy. The facts came to us through her.'

'Facts?' Bob queried. 'I wonder if you realize that Jack Luker let Manderson take the document. Kathy wasn't in the sheriff's office to see or hear any part of what happened there. I doubt her pa would have crowed over Luker's part. He must have some loyalty to the varmints who give him what he wants.'

'Luker's gone,' Ray said. 'He rode out of Starrville on the fastest horse that he could buy. He left his missus—left everything.'

'The law can't touch him anywhere,' Bob reflected. 'The cowson was Peter Blood's heir. He deserved to be strung up, but I wouldn't waste my time hunting down fat trash like that. The bastard had been rattling Mary Lewis, and I figure she sort of took the water agreement for services rendered.'

'Kathy had worked it out much like that,' Ray Archer said. 'Oh, I reckon we have a clear enough picture of it, boy. You can't add a lot more to it. You've done your best by us, and had a rough time because of it.'

'Well, I pray God you've got a miracle to come!' Bob said, snapping his fingers impatiently now for the things that his brother had still to supply; and he was about to speak a few sharp words to hurry Ray up, when a cry from

Fergus Dean—who was facing in the same direction as Archer, which was the opposite to that in which all the other men drawn up there were facing—caused him to snap his mouth shut and glance away to his right where, at an angle of about thirty-five degrees, as the young landsman was lifted up in his stirrups and pointing out, the night sky was even redder than it was above the nearer end of the town.

'Miracle!' Fergus Dean howled out in horror. 'It appears to me we've got a disaster instead! If that ain't fire yonder, I never saw it!'

'God a'mercy!' another man cried on craning about. 'The boy's right. Them's our farms a'burnin', Ray! Ain't nothin' else over that way to blaze up so!'

'Our women and yunkers!' somebody else literally bawled. 'There's been a massacree behind our backs!'

'Keep your nerve, Parker!' Ray Archer roared. 'If there had been any killing back yonder, we'd have heard the shots!

It's Orv Manderson, rot his heart! He's got that water agreement, and now he's going to treat us like squatters. Them ranchmen must've been bidin' their time—and laughed like hell when they saw us ride out. God dammit! The worst of it is, thereain't no law anywhere that'll stand up for us!'

Bob Archer was shocked and again fighting mad. 'Don't just sit there like addlepated rubes!' he shouted. 'Get your butts back home! Ride, damn you, ride!'

That did it. The men swung their horses round and away they went. The party stretched into gaps, ahead and to either hand. It might have been a race, and yet was so much more. The moon was clear of the horizon and a broad swathe of its pale light hovered on the darkness of the land. Into this pallid glow the horsemen breasted, thundering for broke, and the tubes of the straining horses coughed and whined, sounds which merged with the creaking of harness straps and clinking of bit and stirrup metals—the whole effect forming a ground bass to the music of the night. It was all ride. They made no attempt to travel beaten ground, but cut corners as tightly as they could, and were soon kicking up tilled soil and newly planted seedlings as they approached the first of the strip's farmhouses, which was already blazing at its heart and sending up flames of yellow, green, and bright orange. There was a breeze, and this blew against them. In it Archer could smell dissolving timbers and melting tar, and the fumes from these things caught in his throat and stung his eyes. He judged that it must be the same for every man present, and he cursed the smoke that rolled like a black tide between heaven and earth. Better to fight to the death than choke on these hellish infusions. But there was no enemy around to fight, and the gusty roaring of the fire was almost superseded by the heartbroken calling of a woman and the wailing of children.

A horse surged ahead of the rest. It was no great shakes as a beast, but found its turn of speed in a goading that went beyond cruelty. Its master was kicking and lashing at it in what amounted to a display of outright madness. In fact the man almost pulled the mount onto its jaw as he swerved in close to the weeping female and swung up a leg and vaulted to the ground with a virtually impossible skill which he could never have duplicated. Since this man was doubtless the husband and father here, Archer expected him to sweep the woman into his arms and do what he could to comfort her—for it was plain that her entire home was past saving—but such were the horror and confused emotions of the moment that the man stood over the quaking female and railed at her, while two small children ran back and forth between them finding comfort in neither.

Then Ray Archer reined back almost to a halt and shouted: 'Cut that out, Parker!

There's nothing you can do here! Come on with the rest of us! You may get a gutful of revenge down the road! Don't you want it?'

The man gaped at the speaker, seemingly an entangled shape amidst the whirling reflections of the fire, and then, ignoring the pleas of the woman, he sprang back on to his drooping horse and turned the animal's head to the right, soon rejoining the charge across country from which he had broken away and heading eastwards for the next farm in line across the strip, where the pulsing vividness of another conflagration was already in sight.

They neared the second farmhouse, and the events which had occurred outside the first were to some extent repeated—allowing that the evicted occupants were of a slightly different temperament and that the shock of gazing upon fiery ruin had now been blunted for the galloping farmers—and here again the landsman involved left his family to suffer and

218

carry on as best they could while he tacked himself again to the tail of his charging fellows and carried on towards the third farm in line.

Here, too, a blaze had got a hold—but was nothing like as advanced as at the two previous homes—and now Ray Archer shouted to the owner of the property, one Ed Malone, that Malone should drop out of the party and see if he could not check the blaze—which four members of his family were already trying to do by tipping water from the rain-barrels on it—or at least try to save some of his more valuable possessions, and Malone waved an arm in acknowledgement and then slanted off towards the back of his patchily burning home, where he vanished into a field of the blackest shadows.

Bob Archer and the remaining farmers went on galloping ahead. Presently they closed on the fourth farmhouse. The dwelling had fire licking up from its foundations, but was barely harmed as yet. In fact crouching men were still moving around the building and touching off piles of straw which were apparently soaked with oil and placed at the more combustible points about the place. They had cotton-waste torches flaring in their hands, and it was immediately obvious that they were the fireraisers responsible for all the burning which had so far occurred along the strip. The farmers lifted in their stirrups. 'Get the bastards!' went up the cry. 'Get em!'

Pistols began booming and sprouts of scarlet fire darted across the section of the night sky which held the moon. Bob Archer, like the rest, was riding with his revolver drawn. The arsonists were in range, and one straightened from his task—no doubt on hearing the onrush from the land—and he twisted round, dropping his torch in the process and going for his gun. The farmers shot at him there and then, the explosions rippling into echoes—and no doubt some of their bullets went close—but this was Archer's kind of engagement, joined many a time in conditions such as these, and he covered the target before him and triggered. Over went the man missed by everybody else, and he lay motionless.

Not far off along the wall of the house another figure squared into view against the fire that he had just set burning. Archer put a bullet through him, too, and over he went. Smiling grimly to himself, Archer sought a third target. Amateurs, he was dealing with amateurs. Killing the hellions was going to be too easy. If these fellows had had even a scrap of experience in this sort of thing, they'd never have allowed themselves to be surprised like this. Presumably, they had expected the burning of the farms to be almost without risk and that their own inflated opinions of themselves would be a further protection. Archer got his third man at this point and cocked his gun anew. Yeah—this was where that ranch scum learned their lesson!

He guessed the sons-of-bitches would be on bonuses of fifty dollars a man. Not a fortune, but a nice little sum. Enough to provide a dead man with a new suit for his funeral and a properly cut headstone. But, what was far more important, Archer hoped that, in the moment of dying, each of these fireraisers would be aware that the game hadn't been worth the candle. Anyhow, the devil torched souls in hell—not dollar bills!

Lead passed within an inch of Archer's left temple. Then a second bullet whipped at his shirt. It was his turn to feel sobered. Where the heck had those slugs come from? They had been fired by somebody who had kept his head. Whoever the guy was, he was going to kill a farmer or two if he wasn't himself killed first. Inviting another bullet, Archer sat up straight in his saddle and peered away to his left. The gun that had been threatening him blazed a third time, and a slug clipped his left forearm—hurting like hell!—but he had glimpsed his would-be killer behind the gunflash. Now he lined his Colt on the other in the sure knowledge that he was aiming at that old vigilante comrade of his, Dan Burton, who had fired on him yesterday while attempting to drive him off the approaches to the Broken M ranch. After that he called: 'Not again, Dan! Don't you dare!'

The big man made the mistake of firing again—certainly of missing—and Archer shot him in the chest without more ado, then rode straight at his victim's staggering form and knocked it over. He trampled the dead or dying Burton and rode on, resuming his place among the still charging farmers, remarking that his brother Ray seemed to be doing an able job of leading them, and the body of horsemen halved at the command and surged down either side of the newly burning house adjacent, flushing out the fireraisers from every nook and corner in which they were hidden. The men ran hither and thither like frightened rabbits in their attempts to escape, and were gunned down accordingly. It wasn't pretty to watch, and Archer didn't like to see decent men giving themselves up to the annihilation of an enemy, but the kind of villains who burned other people out were a particularly nasty form of vermin and no impartial mind could deny that they richly deserved their fates.

Before long it was done. One or two of the enemy had unquestionably managed to escape. But it was doubtful if this fortunate handful would be heading back to the Broken M and so posing a further threat to the landsmen in the future. They were bullies who had had their backsides well and truly kicked—if that could be deemed in any way a true description of what had taken place—and bullies seldom came back for more.

The riders pulled their horses down to a walk and began to circle rather aimlessly, men waiting for a call to draw them together again. This came when

Ray Archer shouted to them through the fraught silence which had now fallen so suddenly on the Blood country. 'What's it to be, you fellows? We've already played Hob, and I reckon we should make a job of it tonight! I vote we ride up to Orville Manderson's ranch and burn the place down. Sauce for the goose, boys!'

Roars of approval went up and, though he was against the kind of large scale destruction projected here—not least because the Broken M ranch house was blonde Kathy's home and thousands of cattle would roam untended locally if the Manderson organization were totally destroyed—Bob Archer knew that he must hold his tongue and let these men settle this business once and for all as best pleased them. He would look on for as long as he had to, then leave the district as fast as possible. He'd go this instant if he could, but he needed that bit of money from Ray, and the bag of food too.

'Talk up, friends!' Ray Archer bawled.

'Are we all in favour of sending the Broken M up in smoke?'

An affirmative yell answered him.

'Is anybody against it?'

The reply came as an equally loud negative.

'Good!' Ray Archer pronounced with a snap of his teeth. 'If we meet opposition, we'll go over the top of it. We've been shown no mercy, and we'll show no mercy. We'll only return from the Broken M when Orv Manderson is swinging and every last building has been reduced to ashes!'

'That's the style!' the farmers agreed at the top of their voices, for they were clearly taut again and determined to pick up where they had left off down here—regardless of the cost that might one day be exacted from them in a court-of-law.

'Come on then!' Ray Archer cried, going as far as to swing his one good arm in an attempt to create instant momentum; but at that very second a rider came galloping up out of the darkness on the right and there was such an urgency in his clatter that the farmers checked despite themselves and everybody peered intently towards the newcomer.

'Pa! Pa!' a boy's voice called from the back of the approaching horse.

'Harry?' Ray Archer shouted back, a big question in his tones. 'What the deuce are you doing here, boy?'

The youngster skidded his mount to a standstill close to his father's horse. 'It's that Mary Lewis, Pa!' Harry Archer gulped out. 'She's dead! She's layin' on our parlour floor, bleedin' something fearful—poor girl! It was Tug Filby did it!'

'How's your mother then?' Ray Archer inquired anxiously, for there was obviously a great deal more behind the arrival of this information than was presently emerging from the youngster's inevitably skeletal and probably disjointed account.

'That's it, Pa,' the boy said helplessly. 'That's what I've come to tell you about.'

'For heaven's sake get on with it then!'

'Orv Manderson took her away,' the boy responded rather dramatically. 'He took her back to his ranch with him.'

'He did what?' Ray Archer demanded aghast.

'I told you, Pa—he took her away!' the youngster repeated. 'She's his prisoner. What are we goin' to do?'

Ray Archer sat bowed in saddle, head slowly shaking. The dynamic force of a minute ago seemed to have drained out of him completely. It might have been another man sitting there, Bob Archer waited for his brother to recover, but there was no sign of this happening, and he knew that he had to take over here. Not because he wanted to, but because somebody must!

TEN

Gigging his horse into a position of prominence, Archer said with the firmness that years of command had built into his voice: 'I'm sure we know what's necessary. Let's ride along to my brother's place and see what's happened there. If anybody wants to stay on this farm and help the owner of the house put out the remains of the fire, I suggest he does so. Frankly, I don't think you men will be burning down the Manderson ranch tonight, and I won't insult your intelligence by stating the reason.'

'We can all see that,' one of the farmers said. 'All that matters now is to bring Mrs Archer home safe.'

'I'm glad it's been said,' Archer acknowledged. 'It may stop somebody from doing somethin' crazy later on.' He glanced round. 'Harry!'

'Yes, Uncle Bob?'

'Show us the way home, boy.'

'Right away, suh.'

Bob fell in beside his brother Ray. They rode out behind Harry Archer, with the rest of the party moving at their backs. Harry kicked his pony into a canter, and they travelled down the track that bordered the northern edge of the strip and soon reached Ray Archer's farm. From the rear this showed itself as black and intact under the moonglow. This was a relief to Bob Archer, since you could never be sure of where a programme of destruction began or ended when men set out to destroy. Here a property was missed and there a place was razed, with no definite order being followed, but all was well with the Archer farm, and there was still lamplight shining out of the parlour window when they turned into the farmyard and approached the house from the front.

There had been no further talk during the ride, and there was no further talk now. All present drew rein and swung down. Then, with the youthful Harry still leading the way, the men pressed towards the front door of the farmhouse. Harry went in first, and his father and uncle crossed the threshold at his heels. But when only a yard or two into the living room, the boy stepped aside and, head averted but finger pointing, made it clear to all those who were in the position to see that he had earlier given a true account of what was present here. For Mary Lewis lay upon her back near the centre of the room. Her left temple was crushed and blood was still creeping darkly from her mouth and nostrils. Add to this that her eyes were wide open and rolled back and she was not a pretty sight. It appeared obvious that she was dead, and only a brief examination was necessary to confirm this. 'How did it happen, son?' Ray Archer asked, looking round at Harry, while Bob took the antimacassar off the back of the sofa and cast it over the dead girl's face. 'You mentioned Orville Manderson and Tug Filby. Anybody else?'

'Jem Manderson was there too, Pa.'

'I see. Did they come here after I'd gone out?'

'Sure, Pa. A while after. Mary had come first. She was alone.'

'Afoot or mounted?'

'She had a horse.'

'Let him tell it his way,' Bob suggested, sensing that his nephew was not finding the sequences easy to correlate and express.

'I'd like that much the best,' the boy said—''cos, you see, I heard a heap more than I actually saw. When Ma looked out of the window first off, and twigged we had Mary Lewis callin' on us—who she didn't sorta care for anyhow— she figured somethin' bad was in the wind and told me to go an' hide up in the bedroom.

So that's what I did, and listened at the door.'

Harry went on to tell how the women had talked in voices that were very low and fast—and how he had often been unable to make out much of what was being said between them—but he had been able to grasp that Mary had stolen back some important paper or other that Orville Manderson had seized from her earlier in the day. Then Manderson, his son Jem, and Tug Filby, their foreman, had turned up abruptly and burst into the house—apparently having followed Mary down from the Broken M—and Manderson had begun yelling at the Lewis girl who had started shouting in her turn, all about that dad-blasted paper, for it seemed that the rancher was convinced that Mary had carried it down here and that she and Anne Archer had since hidden it up someplace on this property. The cattleman had ranted and stormed at Mary Lewis for several minutes, trying to frighten her into blurting out what he believed she and Mrs Archer had contrived between them, but the girl had refused to say a word.

Then gunfire had started up not so far away, and Orville Manderson had declared that it must be the farmers attacking the men whom he had commanded to burn down the farms on the strip. He also announced his worry that he believed he and his companions no longer had the time left to expend on 'reasoning' with Mary Lewis, and he ordered Tug Filby to get rough and shake from the girl the information that he needed. Filby had apparently waded in and started doing just that—hurting Mary enough to make her scream—and then matters, so far as Harry could tell, had got out of hand and the girl had bitten the foreman in the face. 'I heard Tug cuss like mad about it,' the boy explained graphically, 'and he must have clocked Mary one. I heard her fall with a thud, and then Mr Manderson reckoned she was dead as a doornail. He told Filby all about his ma and pa—but that didn't do much good—and then he reckoned there was no more time left. The sound o' shootin' was getting that close right then. So now he ordered Filby to grab my mother, throw her on to his horse, and take her up to the Broken M.' The boy concluded with a brief description of how he had heard this happen—after which he had run outside and saddled his pony, heading lickety-split then for the noise of the guns and the red glare of the fires to the west of him. 'Next thing, Pa, I was with you.'

'Right, Harry,' his father assured him. 'You've done well.'

Bob Archer nodded his emphatic agreement with that, then said: 'There's nothing for it but to ride up the hill, Ray—though I wish you'd wait behind.'

'Why so?' Ray Archer demanded angrily. 'She's my missus, g'dammit!'

'You convinced those two women hid that document up?' Bob asked. 'It'd most likely be in this room, wouldn't it?'

'Who the hell can say?' Ray returned shortly. 'The boy don't seem sure about all that much. Women are crafty. The thing could be hid up anywhere around.' He frowned. 'What are you after, Bobby? You've got a mania for twisting up every consarned thing!'

'I was just looking ahead and wondering who the hostage might turn out to be if we suddenly found ourselves held up by Broken M guns,' Bob Archer explained significantly. 'Your influence where your wife's concerned is far higher than mine. See what I'm driving at?'

'No.'

'Think about it some more, Ray,' Bob persisted. 'Anne would let them blow me inside out and not breathe a word. But she'd spout like Old Faithful if your life was threatened.'

'I think I see what you're getting at now,' Ray Archer said uncertainly. 'I can't worry about becoming a target. This will have to wash out whatever colour it wants. Sure, there are risks, and they'll have to be accepted. Damned if I'm afraid of a shoot-out—even if I do lack the use of one arm just now. Orville Manderson got licked to a frazzle back there at the Haines's place just now. He can't have many more men in his employ who're willing to stand up with him and risk dying. And don't forget we'll be riding up to the high country with as fine a bunch of desperate characters as you'll find in Texas!'

'I know their worth,' Bob acknowledged. 'Fact is, though, Manderson must be the most desperate guy of all tonight. He's simply got to regain possession of that water agreement now and destroy it. If it no longer exists, he'll have some excuse in law for his fireraising along the strip. If it's still there, it'll stand as the plain proof he's what we all know he is—a murdering landhog!'

'I can hear what you're telling me, Bobby,' Ray Archer said. 'This is no time for another wild charge. We've got to go carefully into whatever we do.'

'Just so long as we don't let ourselves get outflanked in any way,' Bob said. 'If Manderson can put Anne in a position where she's forced to tell where that document is, everything else will go for nothing.'

'True, brother—and don't we all know it,' Ray Archer said shortly. 'Stay here, Harry, and don't you even dare think of following us!'

'What—what about Mary Lewis?' the youngster asked, a quiver in his voice.

'She's never going to rise up again, son.' Ray said. 'If the sight of death troubles you, go and wait in another room. Or out in the stables.'

'All right, Pa,' the boy said, his features crimping dismally.

Bob Archer wondered whether he ought to say 'farewell' to his nephew—since he was fairly sure that, whatever happened up at the Broken M tonight, he would not be returning to his brother's farmhouse in the foreseeable future—but, perceiving that the boy was in a sensitive mood just now and that it would not be difficult to upset him altogether, with results which they could all possibly do without, Bob grinned briefly and flipped Harry a salute. 'Plenty of straw to lie on in the stables,' he said casually, stepping up to the front door—through which his brother and the other men had already passed—then moving down the veranda steps and back into the farmyard, where he located his mount among all the others standing around with reins hanging.

He swung up, as did the fathers and sons of the Blood country about him, and spurred out in front—intending to ride alone—but brother Ray surged up to his near elbow as they turned right out of the yard. Ray was telling him, of course, that the elder brother had got over his recent shock and was in charge again, and that suited Bob very well—since he was riding once more as a man without any real status here—but he probably had more skill in the business of mankilling than all the rest of them put together, and that was the special gift that he was bringing along for all concerned.

The riders rode eastwards along the foot of the ridge which lowered on their left. They moved clear of the Archer farm within a minute or two. Now they came to the landbridge which slanted upwards to the north of them. Turning on to the connecting slope, they ascended steadily and soon reached the Manderson grass. Overhead the sky was clear, and the moon had now risen high enough to wash out all but the brightest of the stars and fill the dark spaces between land and sky with a thin, shivering radiance which threw the contours of the country above into black relief and showed a clear path through the Broken M's calling herds. The smells of clover and gypsum, young and spring-green, were in a breeze which riffled and swirled up here without much direction. The peace of it all was splendid, yet it had an ominous quality too.

The distances involved were not great. Soon the lights of the Manderson ranch were visible just below the top of the rise ahead. At first a voice had spoken here and there among the riders, but now the hush through their ranks was electric. Bob Archer had no doubt that eyes were watching them out of the shadows on either hand, and that word of their coming had already been carried back to the ranch house. Then there was proof of this, for people began to move like wraiths in the wide band of obscurity ahead, sometimes seen but often not. The whole thing had a medieval quality about it. As if the battle lines were being drawn up.

Archer remembered that his revolver needed reloading. Controlling his horse with the knees, he drew the weapon and extracted the shells from its fired chambers, replacing them with live ammunition from his belt—glad that his brother's gun was of the same forty-four calibre as his own had been. Then, as he shoved the weapon back into leather and picked up his reins again, his brain came abruptly to life. It appeared that Orville Manderson was going to try to face them down in front of his home. The test, then, was to avoid casualties among the farmers during the confrontation or, if casualties there must be, to keep them as low as possible. Archer's mind was fairly racing now. His brother's people needed what was known as an 'edge', and he believed that he could supply one. For Orville Manderson could hardly have heard as yet that he had been rescued from jail—and, even if by some remote chance he had, would not be expecting to find the fugitive among the riders coming up from the Blood country to challenge him in the matter of Mrs Archer—so the man would suppose that he was dealing with Ray Archer and the farmers alone. Allowing for that, it was easy for Bob to see himself as the trump card—or at least a figure who might possibly turn the tide of events by a surprise appearance on the side of the landsmen when least expected. It had to be worth the try, and he felt pretty confident of it. 'Look out for me, Ray,' he said, starting to drop back through the horsemen who were trotting along behind them. 'I'll be there when you need me.'

Ray nodded jerkily, hardly seeming to hear him—much less to grasp what he had in mind—but Bob had no doubt that his brother would think it out over the half a mile of ground that still had to be covered between here and the ranch yard. Jockeying now, and almost at a standstill for a moment, Bob Archer let the party's forward motion take its riders clear of his presence, and then he drew to the left—keeping himself as inconspicuous as possible—and slipped away into the sea of gloom to the west of him, using the cover of the land to enhance that of the night as he presently swung into the north again and headed more or less directly for the ground in front of the entrance to the Broken M, where he could now make out a short line of armed men standing at the ready.

As was to be expected from their different modes of approach, Ray and the farmers were now much closer to the Manderson line than he and, though Archer was reasonably sure that Orville and Jem—who, mainly due to their superior height and holding Anne Archer prisoner between them, were prominent at the centre of the line—would not open fire themselves or command others so to do, you could never be certain what might occur to precipitate violence in a case like this, and it wasn't until the men from the Blood country had halted their mounts and Ray Archer and Orville Manderson had begun to exchange words in a reasonable state of restraint that Bob felt convinced that he would be able reach the position of greatest advantage before anything happened to bring about a perhaps disastrous exchange of fire. It needed only a mistaken movement—or the wrong words spoken between hotheads—to plunge both sides into catastrophe and leave almost nothing to be saved in the end. In that minute the entire world seemed to be walking on eggshells!

Archer was forced to close in upon the main protagonists of the moment much faster than he had intended. This could have proved fatal to both him and his plans, but the men supporting Orville Manderson were listening so carefully to his dialogue with Ray Archer that nobody detected the movement to their right and thus failed to see Bob approaching. Then, deeming that he was now in effective range, the younger of the Archer brothers decided to delay no longer—reckoning that the salvation of all concerned lay in getting this over fast—and he drew his gun and rapped out: 'Let the woman go, Manderson, or I'll blow you in halves!'

'What the—!' Manderson spluttered,

peering through the ashen moonlight with an intentness that held him rigid. 'You!'

'Yes, me!' Bob Archer agreed. 'I'm real, and so's this gun. You heard me! Let my sister-in-law go—or you're a dead man!'

'No, that's what you are!' Archer heard the voice of a second newcomer shout, and he glanced swiftly to his left and saw Tug Filby sitting a horse not a dozen yards beyond him, rifle against his shoulder and sights lined up.

Sudden death, sudden glory was Archer's thought in that awful moment, and he could do nothing but wait for the bullet to strike; but a slightly more distant rifle went off first and Filby nosedived out of his saddle, firing wide of his intended victim as he fell. Then he lay with his face in the grass, strangely hunched, and there was no further movement from him.

'Do for him, Jem!' Orville Manderson shouted in his son's ear, and the two men swung on Bob Archer with their pistols cocked and rising.

Recovering almost instantly from the shift in his attention, Archer snatched his gaze round to meet the new threat. He received a fleeting impression of his sister-in-law leaping away from her captors as their guns went off. Braving the bullets—which missed him in both cases by the tiniest of margins, perhaps because of the woman's unsettling movement close to the shooters—Archer held himself erect in the saddle and began fanning his hammer. His revolver bucked and roared in his grasp, fire spitting from its muzzle and chaplets of gunsmoke pulsing away from the flames, and the thunder of the explosions continued until the only sound which issued from the weapon was an empty clicking. Now Archer stopped chopping at his pistol with the side of his hand and looked at what he had done. Both Orville Manderson and Jem, his son, had collapsed upon the grass and were lying inert. Steadying his horse, Archer prepared to dismount and inspect his fallen enemies, but he saw at once that there was no need. Other men had already run forward and were crouching over the riddled pair, and it was one of the Broken M employees who looked up and round and declared: 'That was some shootin,' mister! They're both dead as mutton.'

Archer nodded curtly. It had had to be done. The bad inevitably came to bad ends. But it was no good dwelling on the obvious. Life went on, and tomorrow was another day for the living. 'Anne!' he called to his sister-in-law. 'Where did you and the Lewis girl put that water agreement?'

'I didn't put it anywhere, Bob,' Anne Archer replied. 'Mary left it out at Cold Wells. She told me it's lying under the only white rock there.'

'That's plain enough,' he commented. 'Ray will know where to find it then. I believe your troubles are over now on that score.'

'You can depend on it!' Kathy Manderson's voice announced, as she rode slowly in from the gloom that stretched to the west of the ranch yard, a still smoking rifle held in her right hand and propped on the front of her saddle. She stopped just short of where the bodies of her newly dead father and brother lay, but did not look down at them as she went on: 'I saw the fires on the Blood land from town, and knew I'd be needed up here. Well, it's done, and the Broken M ranch appears to be mine now. All I want in future is to live in peace with everybody here. If anybody has a quarrel with me or mine, I hope they'll bring it to my office and say what they want to say. I promise to listen. I'm not going to be a soft touch or an easy employer, but I will be fair.'

'That's the most anybody is asking, Kathy,' Ray Archer said. 'If you treat us right, girl, we'll do the same by you.'

'Give me your hand on it,' the blonde said, 'and we'll seal the bond of friendship for everybody here.'

Ray Archer moved his horse up level

with the girl's and they shook hands.

'Thanks, Kathy,' the watching Bob Archer said—'for everything. Especially Tug Filby.'

'Can't you stay, Bob?' Kathy asked wistfully. 'The place could do with you.'

'You know I can't.'

'Yes, I do,' she admitted. 'Buck Stevens isn't worth a bucket of spit, but he's the law. Folk forget the good we do, but they never let the wrong go away.'

'Ain't that the truth!'

'Another lifetime?' she queried enigmatically.

'Sure,' Bob said. 'See you then. Look out for me.'

'You goin' to talk all night, son?' Ray Archer inquired. 'What are you hanging about for?'

'A bag of grub and a few dollars.'

'Ah, yes,' Ray Archer said. 'Seems to me I've still got both with me.' The bag of food he lifted off his saddlehorn and the money he dug out of a trouser-pocket.

He handed both over to his brother. 'You write now. Don't you forget us.'

Bob Archer lifted a hand, then spurred off. He was heading for the North Star.

This Large Print Book for the Partially sighted, who cannot read normal print, is published under the auspices of

THE ULVERSCROFT FOUNDATION

THE ULVERSCROFT FOUNDATION

. . . we hope that you have enjoyed this Large Print Book. Please think for a moment about those people who have worse eyesight problems than you . . . and are unable to even read or enjoy Large Print, without great difficulty.

You can help them by sending a donation, large or small to:

**The Ulverscroft Foundation,
1, The Green, Bradgate Road,
Anstey, Leicestershire, LE7 7FU,
England.**

or request a copy of our brochure for more details.

The Foundation will use all your help to assist those people who are handicapped by various sight problems and need special attention.

Thank you very much for your help.